"Roman, there's some

"Where are you?"

"Locked in the bedroom with Ian," Emery said.

"I'm five minutes out. Make that three. Stay on the line with me."

She heard the revving engine, imagining she could detect Wally's slobbery panting in the passenger seat. Trying hard to quiet both the baby and her own breathing, she strained to hear any sounds from outside. Were those normal shadows writhing outside the curtains, or someone approaching? It was as though she were being tossed in the river all over again, helpless, drowning... Roman's voice on the phone snapped her back to the present.

"Are you hurt? Ian? Where's Gino?"

"We're okay. I don't know where Gino is. Ian's crying because I woke him up. I was in the basement and..." She froze as a human silhouette glided across the closed bedroom curtains. "Roman," she whispered over her thundering heart. "I think there's someone walking outside."

"I'm almost there. Hold on."

Dana Mentink is a nationally bestselling author. She has been honored to win two Carol Awards, a HOLT Medallion and an RT Reviewers' Choice Best Book Award. She's authored more than thirty novels to date for Love Inspired Suspense and Harlequin Heartwarming. Dana loves feedback from her readers. Contact her at danamentink.com.

Visit the Author Profile page at LoveInspired.com for more titles.

Tracking
the Truth

DANA MENTINK

LOVE INSPIRED SUSPENSE
INSPIRATIONAL ROMANCE

LOVE INSPIRED® SUSPENSE
INSPIRATIONAL ROMANCE

ISBN-13: 978-1-335-59799-1

Tracking the Truth

Copyright © 2024 by Dana Mentink

Recycling programs for this product may not exist in your area.

For questions and comments about the quality of this book, please contact us at CustomerService@Harlequin.com.

® is a trademark of Harlequin Enterprises ULC.

Love Inspired
22 Adelaide St. West, 41st Floor
Toronto, Ontario M5H 4E3, Canada
www.LoveInspired.com

Printed in Lithuania

MIX
Paper | Supporting responsible forestry
FSC® C021394
www.fsc.org

If ye then be risen with Christ, seek those things which are above, where Christ sitteth on the right hand of God. Set your affection on things above, not on things on the earth. For ye are dead, and your life is hid with Christ in God.
—*Colossians* 3:1–3

To Susan S., a woman of God who encouraged so many.
You will be missed.

ONE

Roman Wolfe lay on his back in the tall grass, cloaked by darkness, invisible. Even the sliver of moon was co-operating, playing peekaboo behind the clouds. He used a special remote to trigger his car to unlock, put his finger to his lips and whistled once, a piercing signal that sliced the winter night in this northernmost fringe of California, a stone's throw from the Oregon border.

It's all up to you now, Wally. Don't let me down.

The lake water rippled, counterpoint to his thoughts. He'd left the two-year-old black-and-tan bloodhound in his car a mile away. Now it was up to the headstrong Wally to let himself out of the vehicle and do his thing. No sweat on the first part. Wally had mastered opening the car door his first day with Roman. After that, the dog had proved difficult to train, but he'd chalked that up to the ownership transition. Wally's first adopter was swept up in the excite-ment and prestige of possessing a bloodhound, without con-sidering the steep challenges of the breed. No blessing is free, his uncle Jax used to say. He dismissed that thought immediately.

He breathed in the frigid air, recalling his days as a navy master-at-arms, patrolling the base in the wee hours with various dog companions. Those days were full, planned, monotonous sometimes, but always purposeful. His seven months as a civilian had been an adjustment when he'd come home to Whisper Valley, a skip and jump from Oregon's Crater Lake. Home? *Yes. How long before you finally believe it?* He forced away the uncertainty he'd probably never outgrow.

Home is the people who chose you. He'd been an unofficial part of the Wolfe clan since he was a sixteen-year-old runaway. Beth Wolfe had officially adopted him when he'd returned home on leave on his birthday at age twenty-two. It was still surreal. He'd blubbered like a baby. How many people actually got adopted as adults? Plenty more, if Beth Wolfe had her way.

"You're a Wolfe now," she'd said with tears in her eyes.

Part of the pack. Now he and his adopted siblings all worked for the fledgling Security Hounds investigation business, Beth's dream. He'd made it his dream too.

He cocked his ear at a sound. Wally? No, surely not yet. It was coming from the direction of the lake. A motorboat at this hour? He could check the time but he didn't want to give Wally any help by way of a light. Not that it would matter since Wally was scent-driven, basically a nose with a dog attached. Still it had to be closing in on midnight. Roman had chosen the ridiculous hour so there would be no possibility of interruption from a fisherman or hiker and no danger if the dog went wandering instead of completing his training exercise.

The nearest road was a mile away, which was important since Wally, like all their other bloodhounds at Security Hounds, had *zero* street sense. Put an interesting odor in front of that dog and he'd scamper across a six-lane highway without a backward glance. Typical bloodhound, except for the fact that Wally was proving to be much less interested in doing his job than his canine counterparts. Each one of Roman's four Wolfe siblings was teamed with a highly trained bloodhound, which they deployed when needed in the course of their detective duties.

But Wally? It was looking like he was going to be assigned to the couch to nap and nowhere else if he didn't start shaping up.

The quiet washed over him again, along with the chill. The January temps in this untraveled section of Whisper Valley were generally enough to discourage casual outdoorsmen, but there were diehards, like himself and his brother Garrett, who might be out and about at such an odd hour. He breathed deeply of the pure night air. Whisper Valley was a phenomenal place to raise and train champion bloodhounds…and to headquarter an exclusive investigations business. And an excellent place to call home, if he could only make his heart accept it.

He mentally ticked away the moments while listening for the odd boat noise, which he couldn't dismiss from his mind. Someone night fishing? In January? With a motorboat? Maybe it was his navy training that made his instincts prickle. That and the fact that they'd already seen a lot of weird stuff in their inaugural year in the investigations biz.

He batted a flying insect away from his buzz-cut hair.

Why don't you let it grow out? his sister Stephanie always suggested.

He'd told her he liked the low-maintenance cut, but it was an evasion. He buzzed it because it was red and he'd been constantly teased in school, in his half dozen foster homes, at work, until the moment the military had shaved it off for him, like they'd detached him from his less than stellar past. *Thank you, Navy.*

Pain stabbed at him, but it was not the pain of leaving

the military six months prior. He'd been ready to start a new challenge. It was the pain of betrayal from the man who'd pointed him to the service, after whom he'd modeled his life, the one who'd made him believe in himself again: Theo Duncan. Theo, who'd confessed to shooting and gravely wounding an unarmed man.

The invisible knife gouged his gut again. God had shown Roman one more time that he had no reason to trust any man alive and no woman either, for that matter, except Beth Wolfe and her other four children.

A splash...louder now. A fish? Trout could get to be a pretty hefty size, which could account for such a noise. He sat up and checked his precision watch. Wally should have found him by now. Another failed mission. Why would this dog not do the job for which he was born and bred?

His phone vibrated.

"Well?" Stephanie said.

"Wally's a dud. He only finds when he feels like it."

"Wally is sensitive. He's had a rocky start. Besides, you offended him by making such a big fuss about breakfast yesterday."

"He literally snatched the scrambled eggs and hash-browns off my plate in the space of thirty seconds. He'd been planning the whole theft, waiting for me to turn around to get the ketchup from the fridge." Roman realized he sounded ridiculous.

"At least he left you the fried tomatoes."

"Good thing he doesn't like tomatoes or I wouldn't have gotten those either." There was still no sign of the gangly hound galumphing through the grass. He wouldn't admit it, but he was beginning to worry. He checked the GPS tracker affixed to the dog's collar. "Unbelievable. He's still sitting there in the car. He hasn't even budged."

Stephanie's guffaw was so loud he had to hold the phone away from his ear. "I cannot wait to tell everyone about this."

By dawn, Stephanie would have told the rest of his siblings. Chase, Garrett, Kara and even Beth would be enjoying his failure. He couldn't help but smile. They were the only people he'd ever allowed to laugh at him, which gave him permission to laugh at himself. "I need to go back before he decides to try to drive the car himself."

"Might be a better driver than you."

"Funny. We'll talk later about assigning me a different dog."

"Don't think so, bro."

He forced back the frustration. "I can't work on cases unless I have a reliable dog."

"Wally can't get enough of you. He wouldn't survive the breakup and he's already lost one owner. Besides, we have a big event to prep for, remember? Not the time for changes." She disconnected.

Roman brushed a wet leaf from his ski cap and took a step. Now he heard distinctly the whine of a motorboat in the still air. Maybe a muttered oath? As if the person was struggling with the engine? Rising hairs tickled the back of his neck. He considered. Mind his business and hustle back to Wally? Or satisfy his curiosity and check out the lake?

One more glance at the GPS assured him that Wally wasn't going anywhere. He might as well indulge in a little field trip. He shouldered his pack. The night was dry, at least. A recent rain had softened the ground so he avoided a spot of mud as he jogged toward the water, an easy path that ended in a stop at the bluff where he could get a vantage point. The lake was fed by river water that traveled from Oregon's Upper Klamath Lake and pooled and glimmered below, deep and still.

Until he caught the gleam of a boat bobbing on the surface.

From his backpack, he fished out a pair of night-vision binoculars.

He almost dropped them in shock as a woman leaped from the bow of the boat.

No, not leaped, his brain corrected. She'd been thrown.

And he'd gotten a millisecond glimpse of her hands outstretched, bound by a thick strip of tape.

Roman grabbed his pack and took off at a dead run.

Cold slammed Emery Duncan like a collapsing brick wall. Seconds ticked by. As she swam into consciousness, she struggled to process the screaming messages from her body. Her senses were fogged, thick and slow. At first the only thing her brain could interpret was intense discomfort, of being frozen an inch at a time, a presence all around her, thick as her fear, like being swallowed in a wet gulp. *You're in the water.* Panic choked her as she struggled to figure out which way led to the surface. Why couldn't she see? Move her arms? Her lips were held shut. Terror spurred her to jerk and thrash. A breath, that was the only thing she was fighting for, one single breath. She writhed like an eel.

Her head broke the surface and she tried to gulp in some air, realizing that her mouth was sealed with duct tape. Water burned her nose as she inhaled. Her feet and hands were also bound tightly together. Helpless, she tried to stay afloat. Still she could see nothing. Now she understood her eyes were covered by a soggy piece of material. She reached her tethered hands to try to shove the blindfold aside. It was too tight and she only succeeded in crumpling it enough that she could detect the barest sliver of darkness. Again she was sinking, the water lapping her chin and edging closer to her nose.

Was she in a pool? No, the water was far too cold and she caught the fetid smell of vegetation. How had she gotten here? Slowly her brain provided a spark of memory. She'd been thrown from a boat only a moment before the engine had sputtered off. It must still be close by.

As she fought down the panic, she could detect no sound of the motor over her thrumming heartbeat and the wind-rippled water, only a muffled clank as the captain tried to restart the craft. A new level of fear threatened to overwhelm her. As soon as her attacker got the boat working again...

God, please... She didn't want to die, her life silently pushed out by the water filling her lungs, swamping her senses. Again, she struggled to float away from the vessel, her bound hands and feet working against her. Her father had told her many times about the navy training he'd done as a much younger man. *Slow is smooth, smooth is fast*, she could almost hear him say.

Immediately she stopped thrashing and eased onto her back. Floating, more or less. If she could figure out which way to shore... Ripples of wind driven water broke over her face. The strong smell of wet earth made her nostrils flair. Left, she decided. Solid land lay in that direction. If she wriggled and dolphin-kicked, she might make it.

No, she *would* make it. Theo Duncan didn't raise a quitter, no matter his own tarnished legacy. After pulling a breath through her nose, she oriented herself toward what she believed was the edge of the pond or lake. It was a matter of making slow progress while her attacker was busy with the boat, resting when she needed to, as long as it took to get herself to a depth where she could stand. She wasn't going to die, not now, not this way, with so many unresolved issues in her life. Not with Ian depending on her. Was that a motor sound?

One awkward kick sent her floating along. Another kick and she was getting some momentum.

You got this, Emery. Whoever had thrown her in would have to jump in himself to get to her. As long as she kept moving away she might make it.

Then she felt movement near her. She froze.

Splash. Not a rodent or fish. The two-footed kind of animal.

Someone was coming for her, closer and closer. Though she hadn't detected anyone leaping from the boat, it must be the person who'd dumped her in the water, who wanted her dead. Or an accomplice. Her scream was trapped behind her taped lips.

Desperately she tried to shove herself farther toward land, but a splash of water broke over her, burning her eyes and nose, leaving her momentarily unable to breathe. There was no option to keep it slow when she was going to be caught so she thrashed for all she was worth to get away from her pursuer.

The effort was futile, but she fought on until she felt hands pulling at her. She struck out, but her wrists were captured in a large calloused palm. Only one more chance left. She stopped wriggling, let him get close, and then slammed her head forward as hard as she could. Her move hit the mark, and in spite of her own pain, she rejoiced when she heard a male grunt. She was released.

The celebration lasted only a moment. Then he was reaching for her again, tearing at the blindfold. A man's face appeared, indistinct in the cloud-filtered moonlight, and so close. Where had he come from? The boat? She tried to thrash away.

"Shhh," the man said. "Guy's still out there but he's having motor trouble. Hold still, would you? You almost broke my nose. I'm trying to help."

Help her? She scanned frantically. She was in a lake or maybe a pond, quiet and overgrown. No nearby cars, no civilization. What were the chances this stranger just happened to be in the area when someone was doing their best to kill her? She reared back as he reached for her.

"I'm a good guy, mostly." The whisper was deep and commanding. It felt as if she'd heard it before. "I'm going to untape your mouth if you'll let me."

Let him? What choice did she have? She remained taut as wire while he peeled the tape away from her lips. It left them raw and torn.

"Stay still. I'll tow you to shore."

"Untape my hands first." At least she could defend herself from him...or anyone else.

"I have a knife in my backpack and I can cut you loose on shore. You're getting close to hypothermic. Priority one is getting out of the water before the guy gets his motorboat back in action."

She wanted to resist, to insist that *he* do as *she* wanted, but she was so cold it felt as if her heart might not continue to beat. *Who are you?* All she could make out was a set of wide shoulders, close-cropped hair and heavy brows crimped with concentration or maybe suspicion. At the moment it didn't matter who he was. This man was all that stood between her and certain drowning.

Still her nerves hopped like frogs in springtime. "He tried to kill me."

"Float on your back. We'll move faster."

On her back? She knew she had to trust this man but it was difficult to put herself in such a vulnerable position. "I…"

They both jerked as a motor sputtered to life.

She tried again to yank her wrists free of the tape but it held fast.

Helpless was her first feeling.

Terror was the second.

TWO

Roman twisted to track the shadow of the motorboat speeding across the water. The searchlight fixed to the bow blinded him. He swam between the woman and the oncoming boat. Bound as she was hand and foot, she wouldn't be able to escape to shore, even with Roman's interference. He had to take a chance.

"Stop!" he shouted. Maybe the guy would back off if he knew his victim wasn't alone anymore.

The harsh light almost blinded him, but he snagged a quick glance at the woman who was mercifully still treading water. Seconds ticked by and the vessel churned forward, engine obscenely loud. It did not slow.

He heard her scream for help. Waste of breath. There would be no one anywhere close. No option but one. Time to play offense. He'd been doing that since he was a kid. The boat was close enough now he could almost make out the silhouette of the person standing at the wheel. Close-fitting hat, jacket, face swallowed up by darkness. A mask? Gloves on the hands?

A moment longer…

The boat continued to plow straight at them.

When the vessel was only a few feet away, Roman surged to the side and grabbed the starboard gunnel. His weight hauled the boat low, jerking but not slowing it. He yanked with all his strength and got one leg over the side. One more hoist and he'd be aboard and the moment after that he'd take control of the situation, pull the kill switch cord, stop the boat, deal with the driver.

Too aggressive, he heard Theo, his former mentor, say. *That's what gets you into trouble.* Yeah, well Theo should have followed his own advice. The boat swerved as the driver twisted the wheel. The sudden motion bucked Roman back and he grappled for hold. The aggressor swung out a hand, curled around a sharp blade.

He deflected the blow away from his face, but the blade nicked his forearm. The cold delayed the pain and Roman didn't lose his grip on the side. His weight caused the vessel to veer off course in a wobbling orbit. At least he'd bought the woman more time.

Grabbing at his attacker, he got a handful of jacket and pulled. The knife skittered loose and he heard it clatter to the boat's keel. The attacker came up with an oar and smashed it down a second after Roman pulled his fingers away. The sound clanged through the night, the oar impacting metal instead of flesh and bone.

He regrouped and tried again to heave himself over. This time the oar caught him in the throat.

Gagging, he toppled backward with a splash.

"Look out," he heard the woman shout, but he was struggling for breath, trying not to inhale the water while keeping himself afloat. The driver cranked the throttle, spun the wheel and bore down on him. He was out of options. He'd have to hope he was fast enough to get out of the way and try to reboard in spite of his bleeding arm and labored breathing. Chances were slim to none. He hoped the woman would at least make it to shallower water, maybe hide in the rushes, or scream for all she was worth. Fury bit him like a viper.

There was a mighty splash from the direction of the shore. His pulse roared in his ears mingling with the sound of…barking? Incredulous, he saw Wally churning through the water, enormous ears flapping like sails, moving with all the ferocity of a charging rhino.

"Wally, retreat." He didn't want Wally running into the attacker's knife or getting his skull cracked open by an oar. But his words were drowned out by the barking.

Wally foamed the water as he careened straight for the boat. His big front paws made contact with the stern. He heaved his unwieldy body upward. The dog was actually attempting to climb aboard. Roman commanded him again to desist but there was a high-pitched protest from the throttle as the driver put the boat into Reverse. Wally was shaken loose and fell back into the swirling lake. He barked at a deafening volume until the boat vanished from sight.

After one final earsplitting howl, Wally spiraled around and swam for Roman. He flopped his big paws on Roman's shoulders, swabbing him all over with a sloppy pink tongue. "Easy there, Walls." Roman was still breathing hard. His knife wound was leaking blood into the water. He was relieved to see over Wally's flank that the woman had managed to get her wrists free somehow, her expression mirroring his own incredulity.

"You done good, boy." Roman hugged the hundred-thirty-pound baby. Wally whined and tried to stick his egg-sized nose in Roman's ear, but Roman eased him aside. "Reward time for you later, I promise. We got a situation to deal with right now, big fella." Wally managed to get in one more massive lick under Roman's chin.

They swam to the woman who was shivering violently. Wally shoved his saggy face in hers.

"You're a hero dog." Her voice was high and shaky.

Wally shook his ears as if to agree.

She eyed Roman's torn sleeve, flesh gleaming white in the gloom. "You're cut."

Her voice sounded so familiar. Odd. "Minor. Got to get out of here before boat guy comes back. Someone wants you dead. Know why that is?" Not the time for interrogation, he chided himself.

When she didn't reply, he extended his uninjured elbow toward her, but Wally inserted himself right next to her. She held onto his harness and the dog immediately paddled toward the bank, easily towing the woman in his wake. Roman could only shake his head.

"So you won't follow a scent like you're 'sposed to but you'll carry out a full-blown water rescue operation?" he muttered. Wally sailed along without hesitation, his long tail like a rudder. Bloodhound bodies were not built for aquatic pursuits, but Wally didn't seem to know that.

With one last look around for any sign of the motorboat, Roman swam along behind them trying to let his uninjured arm do the lion's share of the work. The woman let go of Wally's harness as the water shallowed out. She hopped over the mud onto semi solid ground and fell to her knees. He slogged out after her and they were both treated to a sprinkle bath as Wally shook the moisture from his coat.

Roman's arm began to sting and he noted the blood was trickling from the wound. That could wait. He eased close to the woman, careful not to spook her. She was picking at the tape that encircled her ankles. He fished a penknife from his backpack and cut through the restraints before he pulled out a silver emergency blanket and offered it to her.

Trying to keep his cell phone dry, he dialed his sister and continued to watch for signs of the returning boat.

"No signal. Must be in a dead spot. Can you make it to my car? It's about a mile from here. I'll keep trying to call as we go."

Her teeth chattered. "I can make it."

"Injured? Bleeding at all?"

She shook her head. "No."

"Who are you?"

"Emily," she said after a moment of hesitation. "Emily Bancroft."

The name wasn't familiar. Why did she remind him of someone? He pulled a roll of bandages from his pack and awkwardly tried to apply one to his arm. He was about to use his teeth to help rip the packaging when she reached out and did it for him. Her fingers were trembling, but long and elegant, and she knew exactly what to do.

"Medical training?" he asked.

"Traveling nurse, but before that my father taught me the basics."

Nurse. Her father. That's when the pieces slid into place. The familiar voice, slender fingers, determination to do it herself. He stood there, out-and-out staring. She must have realized something was wrong because she gathered the blanket tighter around herself. "What is it?"

"I know you by another name."

She cocked her head, a fleeting sliver of moonlight gilding her heart-shaped face. Her eyes were dark silver but he knew in the daylight they were blue-green. Last time he'd seen those eyes, six months before, they had been unrecognizable, filled with the same disbelief and anguish he'd felt.

"I'm Roman Wolfe." The moment lingered long and taut between them. *Your father was my hero*, his heart added, *until he confessed to attempted murder.* The comment was unnecessary. She knew exactly who he was. They would always be tethered together in the time before both their worlds had tilted.

"You're…" She pulled the blanket tighter. The words dried up.

What was there to say? He felt the yank of guilt in the wake of a fresh stab of betrayal. Her father had wrecked him and he'd about-faced for his own sanity. He'd had no other choice. Not a day had gone by that he hadn't wondered about Emery. Now, here she was like someone who'd stepped out of a dream. "Why are you using a fake name?" He stopped himself. "Never mind. We should get to my car." He hoisted the pack. Wally clambered to his feet and set off down the trail.

After a long moment that made him wonder if she would follow, she hurried after the dog.

Emery Duncan's dad confessed to shooting a man. Now she was going by Emily Bancroft.

Did it have anything to do with why someone had tried to kill her?

Emery settled into the seat of Roman's pristine old Bronco, Wally lolling in the back. She recalled their first meeting, her fifteen-year-old self watching Roman arrive in town, the sixteen-year-old red-haired rebel who worked on the Wolfes' ranch where her father helped out sometimes. Her dad mentored Roman, helped him sign up for the Navy when he was of age. Privately she'd grieved when Roman had enlisted and they'd lost contact.

And she hadn't seen him again.

Until two days after her father confessed to shooting local businessman Mason Taylor at the Taylor estate, where

Emery's sister, Diane, lay crumpled on the lower floor after plummeting from the balcony above.

Theo Duncan's confession was concise. He'd hated Mason's brother, Lincoln Taylor, he said, detested him for the way he'd treated his daughter Diane when she'd shown up with a baby. Diane had been in a relationship with the married Lincoln Taylor. Hilary, Lincoln's wife at the time, was nothing but scathing toward Diane also. Emery understood. Her sister rarely considered the consequences of her destructive actions.

But it was her father who'd confessed to plotting to kill Lincoln and nearly murdering Mason instead. Diane had tried to stop him and she'd fallen. Mason had survived, though he couldn't remember the actual shooting.

Her dad's confession.

The arrest.

Diane unresponsive in a hospital bed.

Diane's three-month-old son, Ian, in the arms of a social worker.

It was all a painful, horrifying blur. One day had bled into the next until the September afternoon Emery had found herself fumbling to unlock the door of the cabin in Whisper Valley where she and Diane had grown up with their father after their parents' divorce. Her fingers refused to cooperate. The keys fell. She'd turned to see Roman Wolfe watching her as she retrieved them. He'd approached in that lanky lope of his that always made her think he belonged on horseback or the heaving deck of a ship. She hadn't even known he was stateside. His civilian clothes confused her.

Emery.

Even before he'd spoken, the question had shone on his face, intense as the beacon on a lighthouse. *"Is it true?"*

She'd known what he meant. *Is it true that your father shot Mason in cold blood?*

No, she'd wanted to say, to shout, to scream. The truth stood between them like a poisonous snake ready to strike.

I read in the paper he...confessed, Roman had said finally.

I don't care what you read. Dad couldn't have done it. Her heart yearned to hear him say he didn't believe it either, that the evidence couldn't be true, that he, like she, stood by Theo Duncan no matter what.

But Roman's expression had shattered, the hurt showing almost as profound as her own.

Almost.

Roman had lost a mentor, a father figure.

She'd lost...everything. She could still hear the rattle of the door after she'd let herself in and slammed it shut against him. Had he knocked, she might have let him in. But he hadn't. And that was that.

Her aching limbs brought her back to the present and she couldn't control the shivering. He cranked the heat.

"The hospital is an hour-plus from here, but Beth is..."

"A nurse, I know." She knew Beth Wolfe, his adoptive mom and a retired air force flight nurse and they'd chatted about the profession. "No hospital necessary."

He didn't look at her. "All right. I'll take you to the ranch."

"I don't need—" She stopped. But what did she need? Her temples throbbed and her thoughts were hazy.

"We'll call the cops as soon as we get there."

She groaned inwardly. The police had done nothing to help uncover the truth about her father. They took him at his word. He'd confessed, after all. What kind of help would they offer her? She wanted to believe he'd been protecting Diane with his confession. Had to be.

He shot a glance at her dark bob, which had been natural blond when he'd last seen her. "You dyed your hair and you're using an alias. What happened?"

A call to his phone delayed her answer. "Steph." He gave her a quick rundown of the situation. "My ETA is twenty." His look slid sideways to her. "She's declining medical transport."

Talking about her as if she were some random accident victim, someone to be dealt with and off-loaded. She was going to insert a remark but fatigue pulled her back against the seat.

When he finally ended the call, he cranked the heat up one more notch. "Police are sending a unit to the lake and then to the ranch."

She wasn't at all sure she had the self-control to keep her temper in check if they started asking about her father. She gritted her teeth to keep them from chattering as they drove. Roman finally pulled the Bronco up the long gravel drive of the Security Hounds ranch.

Before he could help her out, she hopped free, grateful that, though her legs were stiff and her wrists burned from where they'd been bound, she was no longer shivering. The wide front door opened and Beth Wolfe led them inside. Her short blond hair showed streaks of gray, but at sixty, she emanated grace and style in her soft slacks and flowy knit top. There was something hitched about her shoulders though, as if she were experiencing pain. Steph nodded to them, a phone pressed to her ear and a one-minute finger raised. Roman grabbed a cloth and began to towel off the big bloodhound.

Beth led her to a guest bedroom done in soft greens with

oil paintings of Crater Lake on the walls. She gestured to a pair of women's sweats laid out on the bed. "Probably too big since I'm taller, but dry. Are you sure you don't need an ambulance?"

"Yes." Emery spoke a little too forcefully. "I'm an RN."

"I know." Beth cocked her head. "Your father was extremely proud of that."

Her father... She shrank back to the days after his arrest, the looks she got in town, the whispers, the sheer shock of it. Beth had come—in between the reporters who hounded her—walked right past her father's precious geranium patch and knocked on the door. To offer support? She'd been the only one. And Emery had cowered there behind the curtain, face puffed with crying, silent, until Beth had gone away.

Beth left now, without a word, and Emery put on the dry clothes, bundling her own into a soggy ball and leaving them in a discreet corner of the bathroom floor where she could retrieve them later. Why had she let Roman bring her here? But what choice did she have? *Talk to the police, get it over with, figure out your next steps.*

Voices filtered from the living room where Emery joined them. A fire blazed in the hearth and she resisted the urge to sidle up to it. Beth handed her a steaming cup of coffee and gestured her to the sofa. Roman was changed too, into a soft pair of denim jeans and a long-sleeved tee the same cocoa brown as his eyes. His nose was swollen from her head-butting but hopefully not broken.

Then came the questions, delivered politely, from Stephanie, Beth, Roman and Garrett who'd taken up positions in the cozy room.

How had she come to be in that boat?

Who had subdued her and how had they accomplished it?

She heaved out a breath and faced them, putting into words the frightening truth. "I don't remember."

Stephanie quirked a perfectly shaped brow. Her twin brother, Garrett, mirrored the expression. Unnerving.

Garrett poured himself coffee. "You were going by a different name? May I ask why?"

She heaved out a breath. "It's complicated. Can we stick to this evening's events?"

Their collected frowns communicated their perplexity, but there was nothing she could do except say it again. "I don't remember how I got to that lake, or who tied me up and threw me in."

Or why...

And that was the worst part of all.

Why had someone wanted to drown her?

And what was she supposed to do about it?

THREE

Roman used all his will not to flat-out gape at Emery. She had no memory of almost being killed? "If you have a head injury, you should be in the hospital."

She ignored him, rolling the mug between her palms without drinking from it. She was thinner than he remembered, the mischievous quality that had fascinated him, missing. The fine blond hair she'd worn long to her shoulder blades was now blunt cut at her jawline, chestnut brown. The blue-green of those eyes though—a melding of spring grass with the cornflower of summer skies—hadn't changed. He forced his gaze away and focused on what she'd revealed.

Steph brushed a palm over Cleo, her highly efficient liver-and-tan bloodhound. He knew she was buying time to process, like he was.

"What is the last thing you *do* remember?" she said.

"I bought chocolate milk just before 11:00 p.m. At a gas station. It was called the Mighty something or other. I made a phone call."

Garrett was already typing in the information on his laptop. "Must be the Mighty Mart. Twelve point two miles south of here."

"Who did you call?" Roman demanded.

She blinked. "A family friend."

"Who?" he pressed. Too heavy-handed.

Her lips thinned and Beth inclined her head slightly, indicating he was pushing too hard, too fast. But why not? She'd be dead if he'd been a few moments later and Wally hadn't decided to show up. He bit back his remark.

"I finished the milk and I was on my way to Whisper Valley. I heard a car behind me and then…" She blinked. "I woke up being tossed into the lake."

Roman repeated the question. "But why were you on your way to town? You moved away, right?"

He saw her throat convulse as she swallowed. "It's not important."

"Yes, it is."

Her left eyebrow quirked at his tone. "Isn't that for the police to decide?"

A world of challenge in that sentence. Why were they badgering her for information? She wanted to know. Beth got to the particulars before he did.

"Apologies, I thought maybe Roman would have told you. Our new business here on the ranch is an exclusive investigative agency we started a year ago called Security Hounds. You were away then, so you likely didn't know."

"I thought you rescued dogs."

"We do, and we retrain them for tracking and trailing, but we keep a team of them here permanently. They help us find people, or things, or answers." She waved a hand at her children. "This pack has skills, as much stubbornness and curiosity as the dogs. It was a natural fit. So we can help you, you see."

"You won't want to." Her voice was hard and brittle like glass long exposed to the harsh elements. "My dad is in custody awaiting trial for the attempted murder of Mason

Taylor as you all know." Her gaze swept the room. "His military buddies have all deserted him too."

Roman's stomach contracted to a fist. He hadn't deserted Theo. Other way around. Not the time to say so. "Doesn't mean we can't help you."

"Not saying you can't. Saying you won't want to." The accusation screwed his stomach tighter.

He hadn't reached out to help her before, not since that day she'd slammed the door. He'd slammed one too, on the man whom he'd trusted with everything, a man who'd burned them both. Theo didn't deserve their help, but Emery shouldn't suffer any more because of her father.

"Your father was—" Beth stopped "—is a friend. He was there for me and the kids when my husband died. He's a good man, deep down. I won't be convinced otherwise. I know your sister was injured the night of the shooting too. How is she?"

"Alive, unresponsive in a long-term care facility. Has been since that night."

Beth added softly, "And the baby?"

Roman's head jerked up. There was a baby? Why hadn't he known that?

"My nephew, Ian. He's nine months old now. I've got custody. Fortunately, a friend is watching him so he wasn't in the car when…" Her hands trembled.

Emery was caring for her sister's baby? As if her life hadn't turned upside down enough.

Emery examined each person in the room but her gaze came to rest on him. "Like I said, I can't remember anything after the chocolate milk and the car behind me except for the question of why I was on my way here. That part I do know."

Silently he willed her to finish.

She lifted her chin, almost in defiance. "Since Dad went to jail…he's refused to see me, talk to me, and hasn't even answered one single letter or call." Her voice wobbled.

He can't face you.

"He had a heart attack a week ago and was transferred to the prison hospital and then to county. I'm told…" She cleared her throat. "He roused briefly, scribbled a message and asked the hospital orderly to pass it to me. He's been unconscious ever since."

Roman's mouth went dry.

She folded her hands in her lap, palms pressed together. "The message said, *go home, Ree Ree*." Her mouth trembled once and then she steeled her expression. "That's where I was going. Home, to his cabin."

She was returning home because of her father's mysterious command, and while en route, someone had tried to drown her. He scanned the faces of his siblings and his mother. He knew what they were thinking, what Emery needed.

Roman's stomach contracted. He believed that God brought him to situations so he could help. But this one… with her, when he had tried so hard to put Theo's horror behind him? He realized his family was looking at him now, waiting for him to take the lead, or turn away. They knew his pain and they wouldn't add to it by making the decision without his consent. That's what family did…what it was supposed to do, strange as it still felt.

He pulled in a deep breath. "Emery, I think you're going to need help recovering the missing hours."

She shook him off. "The cops…"

"Will investigate the incident, but there's a bigger problem at play here."

"What's that?"

"Someone didn't want you to go home."

The light drained from her eyes. "Do you think it has something to do with my father's message?"

"I don't know, but that's what we do here at Security Hounds. We get answers." *We.* It felt so good.

She wasn't going to find the truth by herself, or from the police, he sensed. And if the mess wasn't sorted out soon, the would-be killer might get another chance at finishing what they'd started. He could be cool and professional if it meant he could offer protection. That's what he'd spent his whole career as a navy master-at-arms doing, anyway.

Emery was simply another person that needed help.

But would she accept it?

Looking at her troubled expression, he wasn't sure what her answer would be.

Finally she pulled in a breath. "No, thank you. I appreciate your offer but I am going to stay at a hotel until the police find my car. All I need is a ride, if it isn't too inconvenient."

You're dismissed, soldier.

He was going to argue when he caught Beth's expression. Instead, teeth clenched, he nodded. "I'll drive you."

Save for the small hotel that was closed due to a problem with the plumbing, there was only one lodge close to Whisper Valley, twenty minutes from town. The police reported they wouldn't be able to interview Emery for several hours so she'd left her contact information. No sense loitering around the ranch if she didn't have to.

Roman's insistence on driving her left her uneasy. What were they supposed to talk about?

"You sure you want to stay at the Lodge?" he asked.

"Why wouldn't I?"

"It's owned by Hilary now, Lincoln's ex."

Emery's stomach dropped but she kept her tone level. "Not much choice. Hopefully she won't recognize me." She shifted, eager to change the subject. "So you're a detective now?"

He shrugged. "More of a manager, I think. I'm still learning the detective end of things. Working on boosting the business any way I can. Beth's scheduled for some long overdue back surgery and I want to be up to speed on how everything works before that happens." His voice warmed. "We've got a big publicity event coming up. It's actually…" He trailed off, suddenly uneasy.

She wondered why but before she could ask, she caught the elegant silhouette of the Taylor home against the black sky. Her memories sucked her six months into the past.

Her sister Diane's text… I was all wrong. Need help.

After her initial annoyance and suspicion, she'd messaged her sister. No reply. From a home health visit she was finishing up near Whisper Valley, she'd phoned her father.

Don't call the cops yet, he'd said. *She doesn't need another blot on her record. Not now.*

Not since she'd shown up in town with a baby. Typical Diane. Moving from one trainwreck to another, only now there was a baby involved in the mess. Typical Dad, trying to correct the damage. What if she'd moved faster? Not let her own difficulties with her sister delay her decision-making? Would things have turned out differently that night?

A touch on her hand startled her.

Roman's mouth had softened slightly. "Bad memories?"

"Yes." And before she could stop herself, the words were tumbling out as she noticed a light on in the Taylors' upper story. "I've tried so many times to imagine what happened that night. It's hard to put into words."

His tone was cold. "I understand why you wouldn't want to talk about it."

He understood? Not likely. Part of her didn't want to share further, but she also felt an almost ferocious desire to force him to face what she had, to hear him say the facts couldn't possibly be what they seemed. "The Taylors' security guard found Diane on the ground floor. My dad was next to her with a gun in his hand and Mason upstairs bleeding from a gunshot wound." She jerked a glance at him. "I know what it looks like, what you think, what everybody thinks, but my dad didn't charge in there intending to kill anyone."

"I've read his statement. He was angry at Lincoln for refusing a paternity test, calling Diane names when she threatened to take him to court. He said Diane's gun was at his cabin. When she texted you, requesting help, he took it, planning to threaten Lincoln into accepting the baby. He didn't realize he was confronting Mason, not Lincoln, because it was dark and they look alike. Diane tried to stop him but he shot Mason and she staggered back and toppled over the balcony rail."

"I know that's what he said," she snapped. "But it couldn't have happened like that."

"Why not? His fingerprints were on the gun."

"Yes, his, but not hers. That doesn't seem odd to you? It was Diane's gun, but her prints weren't on it? She carried that gun when she went on night walks, but Dad said she'd left it at his place when she'd visited earlier in the week. That's strange to me since she walked almost every evening."

Roman shrugged. "Lincoln said he was out for a drive. Arrived back to find the cops all over and his brother shot."

She couldn't hold back. "Convenient that he wasn't there when it happened, isn't it?"

"Cops—"

"Roman, my dad must have confessed to protect Diane. I'm sure of it. That's the only conclusion that makes sense."

"So you're saying he lied, then? Diane did it?"

She swallowed and ducked her chin. "He's always tried to help. I know my father and so did you, once upon a time. He mentored you."

Roman fixed his dark gaze out the front windshield. "My bad for trusting him."

The comment cut an angry path to her heart. *Her* bad for thinking this calloused person was the sensitive young man she remembered. With burning eyes, she stared at the Taylor house. Did the events of that night have something to do with her near drowning? Couldn't have.

The newer structure on the property was sleek and substantial—the showroom for the Taylors' classic car collection. There was a banner erected along the fence line with dates advertising some sort of show. A dark silhouette behind a curtain caught her attention. Was someone tracking them as they drove by?

Her imagination, had to be, but the goose bumps remained.

The terrain became more hilly and thick with trees and another fifteen minutes brought them to the inn. The old property had changed hands many times during her childhood years. She hadn't realized Lincoln's ex-wife was the most recent owner.

Since Roman was dead silent, she had plenty of time to observe the upgrades. The rustic building had been renamed The Inn at the Pines. New outdoor lighting picked up the elegant flagstone drive, a freshly paved parking lot, a new roof gilded by the moon. The cabins sprinkled through-out the property had been similarly glamorized from what was revealed by the artful landscape illumination. She prayed there was a vacancy, determined not to complain about the cost, though her bank account was recently de-pleted with the purchase of diapers and baby clothes. Every day she checked the mail with baited breath, praying the insurance company would inform her they were paying for all of her sister's care. Fat chance.

She intended to thank Roman in the car and check in herself, but he was already out, walking to open the door for her. In a flash, she'd done it herself. She didn't want anything from Roman, especially some sort of forced gal-lantry. Roman left Wally in the back seat.

A stately woman in a blazer and silk blouse greeted them, large brown eyes taking in every detail, it seemed to Emery. Hilary, her nametag proclaimed. Emery was face to face with the woman who had just cause to despise Diane.

Her mouth went dry. "I'd like a room please."

"Of course." Her gaze drifted to Roman. "For one?"

"Yes."

"Name?"

"Emily Bancroft."

"All right. We have one cabin available. Fortuitous since there's a car show this weekend and our visitor count is higher than usual." She chatted on about the amenities. Emery felt she could hardly keep on her feet.

"Paying with a card?"

"Cash." She always carried bills since her cards were under her real name. Settling into life as Emily Bancroft felt as if she could give Ian and herself a fresh start. Espe-cially here, so near Whisper Valley, she wanted no one to know who she was, for Ian's sake. Ian... She experienced the customary mixture of anxiety and warmth that came whenever she thought of her nephew.

Thankfully she had emergency cash in her pocket, since her wallet was likely still in her car somewhere. Would it be enough to cover the room cost? Hilary tapped her blunt-cut nails on the gleaming countertop. "There's something very familiar about you."

Probably Hilary remembered her from the newspaper articles plastered everywhere after the shooting. *Beloved townsperson shot by local resident.* They'd included a family picture of Theo, herself and Diane. There was also a strong resemblance between the sisters. Emery fingered her hair, edging back a few inches. "I've got that kind of face."

"Are you sure I don't know you? Maybe from the car showroom? My ex-husband, Lincoln, runs it with his brother, Mason. People travel from all over to see those cars."

"I…" Her words trailed off and she could think of nothing to add.

"Emily just arrived in town," Roman said smoothly. He flashed that charming smile. "But you know me." He introduced himself.

"Oh, Roman. Didn't recognize you with your hat pulled down over your forehead." She smiled. "Your brother I'd identify in a heartbeat."

"Yes, Chase is a gearhead. He'd go the Taylors' showroom every day if he had the time."

Hilary returned the smile. "Of course. I think by this point I've met all your siblings and mother during our planning meetings."

What planning meetings?

"Yes, ma'am." He offered a friendly smile before he turned to Emery. "There's a coffee station in the corner there. I know you could use a cup after your long trip, right?" He turned back to Hilary. "She's exhausted."

Grateful for the save, Emery scurried to the dimly lit corner to pour coffee. Hilary took the cue and prepared the room key. "Go ahead and settle in. We'll take care of payment in the morning. I'm headed to bed now, but my night clerk can assist you with anything." Hilary's smooth brow crimped. "No luggage?"

Only the luggage that's in my missing car.

"Traveling light." She quickly strode out into the chilly night. Roman caught up with her.

He walked her along the flagstone path and up to a rustic chic cabin, then waited while she unlocked the door. The interior was bright and elegant, a small bedroom opening off a suite area, all done in creams with charming woodland scenes hanging on the walls.

He stood like a dark cliff, hands jammed into his pockets. "You sure you're okay staying here? Matter of time before it comes to Hilary who you are."

"I'll be here only for the night. I've still got my secret identity in place." Her smile was brighter than she felt.

"I…"

"Roman, I appreciate what you did for me. You…" She gulped. "You and Wally saved my life. I can't—" *and I won't* "—ask you for any more."

After a long pause, he turned and left. When the door closed behind him, she immediately latched it. The large rear sliding doors looked out on a swath of crowded pines, impenetrable shadows. She pulled the vertical blinds closed and turned on the lamps on the fireplace mantle. Cozy and safe.

Since she had no suitcase to unpack, she drank the rest of the decaf and decided on another shower. No doubt she was paying a hefty sum for the cabin, she might as well get her money's worth.

After checking once more to be sure the doors and windows were locked, she treated herself to the hottest shower she could stand and pulled on Beth's borrowed clothing. Tomorrow.

By then the police would probably have located her car. She'd load up, return to her central California apartment and stay there with Ian. Try to forget she'd ever come back to Whisper Valley.

Her father's command played in her mind.

Go home.

Well, she wouldn't. And he wouldn't want her to if he knew how close she'd come to dying.

Not just dying, being murdered.

She desperately wished she dared call again to check on Ian. It was after 1:00 a.m. so that would be just plain inconsiderate. In the morning, she told herself. Picturing his little double chin made her smile. Every moment with him was still an exercise in terror and joy, but the past few weeks the joy had been winning out.

She'd folded the covers to climb into bed when a squeak made her freeze, sheets gripped in her fingers. The old logs expanding in the moist air?

That was it, no doubt.

Another squeak. Her pulse raced.

What if it wasn't the expansion of wood, but the noise of a footstep on the slatted porch? Barefoot, she glided as silently as she could, muffling a cry when she struck her shin on the edge of a chair.

Now she could hear nothing but the soft whir of the cabin heater and her own harsh breathing. Easing to the front window, she hooked a finger around the drape and peered outside. Quiet and still, a slice of forest punctuated by the soft glow of the office windows in the distance. She could not see another cabin from this viewpoint.

Isolated.

But there was no one there and the door was still firmly locked.

Relieved, she let the curtain fall back into place. She decided to leave the lamps lit in the living area. Like Ian's choo choo train night-light, she thought. Comforting, that was all.

And why not turn on the light on the back porch? It wouldn't disturb anyone else. She padded to the slider and flicked on the light.

A dark shadow was caught in the glow.

Masked, one gloved hand raised to the door handle.

Emery screamed.

FOUR

At the scream, Wally threw up his snout and howled, vibrating the Bronco's windows. Roman was out and running across the parking lot with the dog right behind before the sound died away. *Emery. Had to be.* He stumbled on a rock and almost went down.

He sprinted along the flagstones and straight up to her cabin door, whamming a fist on the wood.

"Emery, it's Roman." He reached for the knob when she threw it open, pale and trembling. Wally didn't wait for an invite. He bolted inside, jowls flapping and rose up on his hind legs to paw her stomach.

"Down, Wally."

The dog ignored him, as usual.

"I saw someone…" she panted, one hand on the dog, and pointed to the rear slider.

He immediately ran outside, phone flashlight activated. No one was there. To be sure, he whistled for Wally who actually obeyed and joined him. Wally's black nose went immediately to the ground, wafting up great gusts, but without a specific scent article, the bloodhound would be pinballing from one aroma to the next with no target. Roman figured he'd at least bark and alert if there was a stranger in the proximity, but Wally seemed perfectly content to nose around the grass and up to the shrubby border where the lawn met the trees. There was no one hiding, of that he was fairly certain. Wally was a trainwreck in some ways but he generally knew when there was a stranger about. A distant engine noise told him how the peeping Tom had gotten away.

Roman hooked a finger through Wally's collar and guided him back to the cabin. He didn't want him to disappear into the forest and be forced to choose between chasing his dog or staying with Emery. They rejoined her in the cabin and she added what she could.

"I don't know if it was a man or woman. I couldn't see the face. But I saw a gloved hand raised as if..."

"They were going to try to open the sliding door?"

She gave one sharp nod.

He considered, thoughts rolling through his mind. Who? And why? The same two questions looming since they'd barely survived the lake.

A knock made her jump. Roman looked through the peephole and opened the door. Hilary's eyes were wide as she took in Roman and the dog he was restraining from slobbering on her.

"What's going on?"

"Possible intruder." To preempt her next question he added, "I was pulling up here to give something to Emily and I heard her scream."

Hilary's delicate brow arched. "I heard a scream too but I wasn't sure where it came from." She looked at Emery. "Tell me."

Emery repeated her story.

Hilary's brows furrowed. "You were mistaken. No one would be skulking around here. It's a quiet area. You were probably mistaken."

"I wasn't," Emery said quietly. "I'm going to call the police."

Her frown deepened. "Is that truly necessary? It'll upset the guests."

Roman stared. Was she kidding? "You've already got an upset guest."

Her lips thinned. "All right. I'll call. They're not quick on response time around here but I imagine they'll get to us when they can. In the meantime…"

"I'll stay here." Roman got the words out before he thought it through. Both women stared at him but he kept his gaze on Hilary in case Emery was about to countermand his bold pronouncement. "On the couch. Your office sign said pets are allowed, right? I'll pay whatever the fee is."

"Well, small pets, sure, but your dog is sizeable and…"

Slobbery was no doubt her next word. "If he damages anything, I'll pay. I'm sure you want your guests to feel safe?" A challenge rang in Roman's tone and Hilary didn't miss it.

She straightened. "Please call the front desk if you need anything. I'm off for the night but my assistant can help you. Of course, when the police arrive, she'll wake me."

Roman slid a look to her feet as she walked out. Walking shoes, jeans, as if she'd been out walking instead of headed to bed. Might Emery's prowler have been the nosy innkeeper checking on her new guest? But why would she?

When Hilary had gone, he locked the door. Jaw set he turned around to find Emery crouched, giving Wally a tummy scratch.

"You're going to spoil him."

"Why did you come back?"

The weight of her stare made him uneasy. He freed the object from his pocket. "Brought you an extra cell phone we had at the ranch until you get yours back. The Security Hounds phone number is programmed in. And mine." His was the first on the list as a matter of fact.

"Thank you."

He expected her to take him to task for inserting himself into her situation. But she continued to focus on Wally, rubbing him down until his eyes rolled in their fleshy orbits.

"For staying here too. It's only a couple of hours until morning or the cops arrive, but it's an imposition."

"No big deal." He felt relieved that she didn't seem inclined to want to fight him. If she'd argued, it would have been a long night with Wally jammed in the Bronco, keeping watch from the parking lot.

The fireplace lamps lent a soft sheen to her hair, which tossed him back to his teen years, landing on a bright spot in a tumultuous ordeal. He didn't recall much about the mother who'd remanded him into the foster care system at age five. Two years he'd remained in the system until his uncle Jax returned from working overseas and took him in. At Jax's place he'd thought he'd finally found a home with his fun-loving, impetuous uncle. The memories turned sour when Jax remarried and everything fell apart for Roman. At sixteen, he'd walked out, landing at Wolfe Ranch where Theo Duncan volunteered. Dark times, pulsing with anger and hurt.

But there was Emery. He remembered watching her and her father standing over a rescued litter of roly-poly bloodhounds. The puppies were adorable, but he was mesmerized by Emery and Theo, their easy relationship, the love they obviously shared. When he left Jax's and he'd shown up at the ranch, Beth had offered him that kind of love, and Theo had too.

His thoughts soured with echoed snippets. Theo's voice...

If a man can't control his fists, he's not a man.

Holding a grudge is like drinking rat poison and waiting for the rat to die.

All of that meant precisely nothing now that Theo had gunned a man down in a fit of anger and unforgiveness. No matter what Emery said, the facts didn't lie. Her father was in jail for attempted murder, where he belonged, but he'd left a lot of wreckage behind for Emery.

Go home, Ree Ree.

What was Theo playing at? Roping her in again after flat-out ignoring her? That thought tormented him as she said good-night and closed herself in the bedroom. He lay on the couch, comfortable enough until Wally heaved himself up too.

"There's no room for you, dog."

Happily unconcerned, Wally settled his bulk over Roman's shins and started snoring in short order. Roman texted Stephanie since she was a complete insomniac and told her what had happened. She texted back.

Emery needs Security Hounds.

She did. And if she'd agree to the help, Stephanie or Garrett could be point person on the case. Roman was squarely focused on the event he had to be sure was a success, the Cars For K-9s show at the Taylor estate. Security Hounds was struggling financially and he desperately needed to prove to Beth that business was picking up or she'd never stop working long enough to have her back surgery. Her pain was a solid punch to his middle and he wasn't sure how much longer she could take it.

What would Emery think if she knew of his partnership with the Taylors?

His jaw tightened. Why should it matter, anyway? Theo'd confessed and left them all to deal with the fallout as best they could. Case closed.

He tried to put the thoughts away and lull himself to sleep.

After what felt like only a momentary rest, Emery was up, dressed and headed for the small coffeepot in the room when she found Wally and Roman entering through the front door. Roman held two mugs of coffee, one of which he offered her. She was glad to see his head-butted nose looked much less swollen in the clear light of morning.

"Got it from the lobby. There was a blueberry muffin too but Wally snatched it from my hand while I was trying to hang onto the coffee. Fortunately Hilary didn't see that little stunt."

Wally wagged his tail at Emery as if he were being lauded by his owner. She giggled.

"Cops called," Roman said. "They can't get an officer here until later but they asked you to meet them at Wolfe Ranch to answer a few questions."

"I want to get back to my apartment and Ian." She sighed and sipped the coffee while Wally sniffed her pant leg. "But I guess I need to give them whatever info I can before I leave."

"Wally and I checked the area this morning. Stayed far enough away not to mess up any footprints, but I don't think there are any. The flagstone butts right up to the patio."

"Hilary thinks I was imagining it."

He didn't reply to that. Did he believe the same thing?

"We can go anytime, Ree. I settled up for your room so you wouldn't have to do a face-to-face," Roman said.

Her cheeks flamed both at what he'd done and his use of her nickname. "Oh, wow. I'll pay you back, whatever it was." Her thoughts raced. How, exactly? She'd had to curtail her work hours for Ian's sake. Her sister's medical bills were mounting and there was a mortgage payment on her father's cabin due, which she had no idea how to pay. Prickles danced up and down her spine.

"Ready to go?"

"More than ready."

They drove back to Whisper Valley and she again found her gaze on the Taylor estate and car showroom. "Why would Hilary take over an inn so close to the Taylor estate after divorcing Lincoln? My sister said it wasn't exactly a friendly parting." Lincoln had been unfaithful to Hilary with more than one woman and Diane was the latest in a string. It made Emery cringe that her sister had been involved in ruining a marriage. How had Hilary felt about Diane's arrival with a baby in tow when the ink on her divorce papers wasn't yet dry?

"The car showroom attracted visitors but there was no place close for them to stay. Hilary and Lincoln made some sort of business arrangement for her to renovate and run the inn so the visiting car enthusiasts would have lodging. You'd be surprised how far car aficionados are willing to travel to take a look at the Taylors' collection." He shook his head. "My brother Chase is a total car nut. That guy would crawl in an engine and live there if he could. Cars are just a way to get from A to B in my view, but he'd probably slug me in the shoulder if he heard me say that."

She slanted a look at him.

"What?"

"It's just…nice to hear you talk about family."

He kept his gaze fixed front. "The Wolfes have been incredible. Better than blood. That's why I'm dedicated to helping Security Hounds succeed." His fingers tightened on the steering wheel and she knew what he was thinking. He'd considered her father family at one time too. The tight line of his jaw communicated what his silence didn't.

I need to get out of here, away from him, back to Ian. Her fingers clenched into a fist. A little while longer, after the questioning, and she'd be gone. The drive seemed endless, though it was less than half an hour, but they eventually arrived back at Wolfe Ranch. Wally trotted off to join two other hounds in digging holes in the large fenced yard.

Officer Dell Hagerty of the Whisper Valley Police Department was already seated in the living room. Emery's head pounded and her body ached from her earlier contortions in the river as she repeated the story, exasperation mounting. "I still can't remember how I got from my car to being dumped in the lake."

Hagerty's suspicion was obvious and irritating. "What I want to know is why would your father tell you to go home?"

"I don't know. I'm sure he wouldn't have if he knew it might have put me in harm's way."

The quirk to his lip increased her ire. What he didn't say was clear. *Your dad confessed to attempted murder. His trustworthiness is nil.* Officer Hagerty had been part of the police team that had investigated, but they'd taken Theo's confession at face value. "My dad took the blame to spare my sister, like I said back then. I'm sure of it."

"So your sister did it and he was covering? Why would she shoot anyone?"

"I don't know. I thought she and Lincoln were amicable

at least." Her last text was confusing, out of the blue. "It could have been an accident." The untenable position she was in...defending her father meant blaming her sister. "Or maybe someone else was involved."

Now they were all looking at her with pity. One gun. One set of prints. One man shot. Precisely two suspects. Her sister or her father. And one big fat confession. Her father couldn't have gunned down Mason Taylor. Her sister's volatile temperament made her guilt much more likely, but Emery didn't want to believe that either. According to their father, she'd changed, or tried to, since she'd had Ian. There had to be some missing piece.

The police had been no help in finding different answers because they hadn't wanted to. Case closed. She blinked back to the present, to the suspicious cop staring at her.

"Your father asked you to come back to his cabin, but didn't tell you why, and on the way you were attacked and dumped in the lake, but you can't remember by whom or how?"

Her cheeks were molten. "Yes, Officer. That's about the size of it."

Hagerty looked at Roman. "Do you have anything to shed light on this? Did you get a look at this boat operator?"

This boat operator. As if she were making it up.

Roman crossed his hands over his stomach. "No, but I can tell you someone was bent on killing Emery and then me for getting in the way. What she said is true, every syllable of it."

She didn't know why Roman was vehement in his defense of her, but in that moment she felt a surge of gratitude.

"And someone was prowling your room at The Inn at the Pines?"

She nodded miserably and let Roman fill in the details.

"She checked in as Emily Bancroft," Roman said, startling Emery. She hadn't remembered they didn't know her alias.

Hagerty's brow hitched. "Why are you using a fake name?"

Her anger bubbled up. "My car windows were smashed in twice after my father's arrest and someone painted *Diane's a tramp* on the side of Dad's cabin. Can you blame me? We're living in the Central Valley now, but it's not that far away that the hatred can't reach us."

Hagerty said nothing.

"I was given custody of my nephew. He's a baby. I didn't want any problems to follow us."

Hagerty nodded. "Fair. I've got two kids and I can understand that." The officer asked a few more questions before he excused himself. "I haven't found your vehicle yet. I'll call you if I locate it after I check out the inn. Where will you be staying?"

"I'm going home to my apartment. Both Dad and Diane are in a hospital an hour from here so I'll check on them on my way back. I'll rent a car." With what money? She had a maxed-out credit card and only a borrowed phone. Plus, she owed Roman for her short stay at the inn.

Hagerty shook his head. "Would you mind staying until I can check the inn in case I need you to point anything out to me? Might take a couple hours since there's only one other officer on duty today besides me."

Her heart sank but she nodded as Hagerty left.

Beth stood. "You can stay here, Emery. For the day or however long it takes. We've got plenty of room. Too much as a matter of fact. Chase is working a case out of the area this week and Roman decided to live in his trailer near the kennels instead of a bedroom in the house so we have a spare."

"Says we make too much noise." Stephanie rolled her eyes.

Roman shrugged. "I like to be close to the dogs, but yes, you're noisy. And your country music drives me bonkers."

Emery was at a loss. "I appreciate it, but I should…" Should what? Her backpack with her clothes was in the car, which she couldn't find, along with her wallet. Renting a vehicle would be expensive and she'd need her license. What exactly was she going to do? Wait there awkwardly on their front porch until the police did or did not find her car? Go back to the expensive inn she couldn't afford?

There was nobody she could call on, except Gino, Diane's old friend, who'd arrived in her life just in time, and he was on baby duty hours away at her apartment. No friends had stuck with her after what had happened. She was entirely alone. The weight of it was crushing.

"Please." Beth patted Emery's knee. "Stay for a while, at least. You look exhausted."

Exhausted didn't begin to cover it. Her mind was numb, body battered, spirit troubled. "I, uh, thank you. You're very kind."

Beth walked her down the hall where she fetched her another set of clothes. "In case you need a change. Here's a bedroom where you can rest or get away from the chaos that is my ranch. Between the dogs and the people, it's rarely quiet."

After thanking Beth again, she felt desperate to talk to Gino, to make sure Ian was all right. She called with the phone Roman had given her but there was no answer. Why wasn't Gino home? Her pulse thudded harder. *He's just taking Ian out for a walk and doesn't hear his phone is all.* She left a message adding that she'd been in an accident the previous day. The bed beckoned but she didn't want to allow herself to be too comfortable. *Not staying. Only visiting.* She settled on pacing away a half hour, wishing she had Ian in her arms. Maybe a drink of water might fill the empty spot.

She heard voices in the living room. Padding softly out, she found Stephanie and Roman deep in conversation. Roman caught sight of her when Wally trundled over to give her a good sniffing as if they hadn't just spent several hours together. She scrubbed the dark patches on his tawny sides.

"Um, hi. I wondered if I could, um, have a drink of water." She felt silly, childlike.

Roman immediately went to the kitchen and returned with a glass. His fingers brushed hers and she felt it to her toes. Nerves.

Stephanie fixed dark eyes on her. "I'm not one to sugar-coat anything so I'll say it out straight. I don't have great hope that Hagerty's going to find much evidence to help here. And your prowler at the inn is likely the same person who tried to drown you."

She groaned. "This has to be a bad dream."

Stephanie perched on the arm of the sofa, unapologetic. "Sorry to be a downer, but there's plenty of wildland around here and Hagerty's got a lot on his plate now that there's another potential crime scene to investigate. Totally your choice to decline the services of Security Hounds and frankly we've got other irons in the fire, but you're making a mistake to go it alone."

"Won't be my first one." Her need to flee was almost overwhelming.

Roman gazed through the window. "Let's give Wally a crack at it."

Stephanie yanked a look at Roman, eyebrows lifted to meet her dark bangs. "Wally the breakfast-snatcher? He didn't even deign to find you last night."

"Until it mattered," Roman said.

Needles of ice pricked Emery's skin. The dog had come through with everything he had. If it weren't for Wally, Emery would be dead and perhaps Roman too.

Stephanie shrugged. "Your sweat equity, not mine. Why don't you take a half a day to work it and if Wally turns up nothing, Cleo and I will take over."

Roman's wide shoulders hunched. "It's Emery's call."

Stephanie rose. "Okay. I'm going to do some background for another case. Let me know if you need me and Cleo." She left.

The silence unrolled between them. The room was suddenly very small.

Roman shifted uncomfortably. "Emery, I know what you told Hagerty, but do you have any idea why your dad would have sent you that message?"

"No."

"No guesses? Hunches?"

"No. I don't understand anything involving my father."

"I don't either."

His bitterness was like a living creature and it awakened a surge of smothering shame. This was why she could not accept his help. Because deep down she knew that she was partially responsible for what her father had done and if that guilt was exposed, especially to Roman, she would not survive it. She'd abandoned her father, left him to deal with Diane alone because she was sick to death of it all.

What's more, she was secretly relieved that he'd responded to her sister's frantic text, which had let Emery off the hook.

Right now, there was only one tiny thread keeping her heart intact, the faintest hope that somehow, someway, her father would reveal another side of the story, one where he wasn't murderous, and Diane wasn't either. A third party… someone…anyone. But Roman would think that was self-delusion. More than likely he was correct. She shook the hair from her face. "I'm leaving as soon as I can. I appreciate the offer, but I'll figure this out on my own."

"How?"

"One day at a time, like I've been doing for six months."

He didn't flinch, didn't look away this time. "You need Security Hounds," he said quietly.

"I don't need anyone." *Just herself, and God.* She remained silent, wishing she could disappear into the floor, out of this house, the town. Roman had once been the center of her teenybopper crush. Now he was a stranger who reviled her father, like everyone else in Whisper Valley. His brown eyes searched hers fleetingly. She kept her chin up, mouth firm. He headed to the front door.

Roman wanted to give Wally a crack at finding her car.

To him, it was a case, one she was sure he didn't even want.

To her…she remembered the terror of waking up bound, gagged and drowning.

To her, it was life and death.

Her death.

And if she were gone…who would be there for Ian?

She felt again the frigid water closing over her.

"Wait," she blurted.

He jerked around. "You change your mind?"

"Maybe it wouldn't hurt to let Wally look. I have to stay in town for a few hours anyway."

He smiled and her stomach tingled. He was older now, his face tanned, worn and more angular, but the smile was the same one she'd briefly lived for as a teenager. She looked away. No time for silliness.

"Great. I'll get Wally harnessed."

She tracked his wide shoulders as he departed. A couple of hours, that was all. What could happen in that time?

A shudder rippled her spine.

Plenty.

FIVE

Roman's mind reeled as he drove. Why had he volunteered, anyway? He certainly didn't want to involve himself in her case. But something in his gut told him his breakfast-swiping dog could find the car. Locate the vehicle. That was all.

"Wally's in training to trail people but maybe we can do some reverse engineering." He pulled to a stop at the lake where he'd found Emery and unloaded the dog, clipping the long lead to his harness. "All right, boy. Let's see if we can make this work."

While Wally nosed around, Roman scoured the ground for something the perpetrator might have dropped near the boat launch. "If we can find a scent article, Wally could theoretically lead us back to the place where you were abducted, providing we've got one attacker here and not two working together." He realized that Emery had stopped several paces behind him, hugging herself.

"Are you cold? I've got an extra jacket in the vehicle."

She shook her head and he saw the gleam of tears. "It's… hard to be back here."

It took a moment to sink in. Mental head slap. He was clueless. Of course, it would be difficult for her to relive being abducted, dumped in the water and left to drown. It was a wonder she'd held it together at all after that trauma. He edged closer. "I'm sorry. I should've thought about your feelings coming back here."

She flashed a shaky smile. "Gonna buy me an ice cream to make me feel better?"

He grinned. "You remember that?"

"Do I recall the time you found me sobbing after Diane ruined my dress the day before the freshman dance? Yes, I do. You got this absolutely terrified look on your face and offered to buy me ice cream if only I would stop crying."

He shrugged. "I'm still prone to panic when a woman is in tears." At least she appeared a bit more relaxed now. "But I never did make good on that ice-cream offer, did I?" And why hadn't he? Because the gap between her sixteen and his then seventeen was huge. Because he was so uncertain, living in a borrowed place with a borrowed family after his split with Uncle Jax. Because she was so incredibly gorgeous then, and now, he realized with a start. "I'll make good on that ice cream soon."

"Sure." She'd heard the offer for what it was—hollow. She moved away from him, hopping over the mucky areas of the bank.

She doesn't want anything from you. That's good. Too messy. "The police have photographed and gone over the area so we probably won't—"

She cut him off. "Look."

Caught in the reeds, barely visible in the tangle, was an oar, no doubt the same one with which the would-be killer had tried to take his head off. "It must have floated to shore and gotten hung up here." He took a photo and pulled out a rubber glove, snagging the oar between two fingertips and raising it just enough to both leave it in place for the cops and allow Wally access.

"Now we've got something. Time to shine, Wall." At Roman's whistle, Wally splashed torso deep into the sludge and inhaled a snootful, nostrils quivering. After a flap of his massive ears, he set off along a muddy track away from the lake.

Emery hustled after them. "The water didn't weaken the scent?"

"Not enough to throw Wally off. It's not a question of can he find the trail, it's a question of does he want to." Roman sighed. "I worked with German shepherds in the Navy and once they understood who was the boss, they were amazingly disciplined. Not so much with bloodhounds, at least this one. He tends to decide which scents he's interested in following."

"Headstrong, imagine that."

Was that a message for him? He bristled until he recognized it was the truth, whether or not he wanted to admit it. Headstrong, quick to offend; he'd read similar on his military evaluations. Both were qualities he'd tried to work on through prayer. Mixed results thus far. The praying had tapered off and pretty much vanished since Theo's confession. Theo, the man who talked incessantly about God and love and grace and forgiveness. Hypocrite.

Stomach sour, Roman let out the leash and Wally pranced along, stopping, sniffing, circling, moving on and off the path. "He's pretty green, but if he can't turn up anything, I'll get Cleo and Stephanie out here."

Wally stopped dead, turned, and stared at Roman.

Emery giggled. "It almost looks like he's offended you're discussing his replacement."

"Sometimes I think he's a better mind reader than a tracker."

With an indignant swing of his ears, Wally bounded

around a turn, pushing through a patch of tall grass overhung with bare-limbed trees. Roman held a branch to the side until Emery passed beneath.

Wally took them to a marshy area where a rickety pier protruded into the water.

"Might be where your abductor put you in the boat. This is a public dock. Anyone could have access. Could be the person noticed someone else's boat tied up here and decided to use it."

She didn't answer and they scurried to keep up with Wally as he trotted away from the dock, into the tall grass.

"We're doubling back toward the highway." In two more minutes, Wally had drawn them near the shoulder of the paved road. The dog stopped and zeroed in on the ground, sitting and looking at Roman for a moment.

"I might have been driving this road," Emery mused. "It's the best route into Whisper Valley." Before she had a chance to add to her comment, Wally was off again, nearly tangling Roman in the long leash.

"He's got something." He jogged now to keep up as Wally charged on. They emerged at the edge of a ravine, cloaked by tangled shrubs. Wally barked incessantly. Roman pumped a fist as they spotted the rear bumper of her Honda jutting from the foliage and two sets of tire tracks. Emery gasped.

"The abductor ran you off the road here. Took you to the dock and launched the boat. Afterward he returned to his own car and left yours here."

When she ran to open the door, he stopped her. "Cops need to photograph. I'll have Steph contact Hagerty now." His mind spun as he dashed off the text. "It looks as though they sideswiped you to force you off the road."

She nodded her head slowly. "I have a fleeting memory of clutching the wheel. That's it."

"Likely you hit your head. The attacker dragged you from the car unconscious and…" *sensitivity, remember?* "…uh, and then you know the rest of it."

There was not much left of the other vehicle's tire tracks except for the deep gouge in the wet earth. Emery craned her neck. "My phone and wallet must be in there somewhere. A small overnight bag too."

Roman set about photographing the car and scene as best he could without mucking up any evidence. He itched to present the findings to Security Hounds. With their combined resources and talents, it would simply be a matter of time before they'd uncover the perpetrator. Pride swelled inside him. Pride for a pack of exceptional people of which he'd become a part. Had to be a product of God's grace and nothing else.

They sat on a fallen tree trunk and he rewarded Wally with a treat. The dog snarfed it in a nanosecond and stared at him intently.

"He wants more?" she asked.

He offered another treat. Wally let it fall to the ground, untouched, and fixed his surly gaze on Roman. He sighed. "No, uh, there's a particular toy he wants, but I'm trying to get him weaned off it."

"Why? I remember when I visited the ranch with Dad, they rewarded with toys sometimes."

"Bad optics." Wally continued to glare at him. He glared back. "You're a bloodhound, and your breed's origins go back a thousand years. Your findings are considered admissible in a court of law. You can't go around whining for that kind of toy. Where's your dignity? Your self-respect?" He offered a sturdy rubber KONG. "How about this one? The rest of the dogs love these things." Wally was unmoved. He stamped one fat paw into the ground.

Emery cocked her head at Wally. "Aww. He did a great job finding the car. Besides, if you don't give it to him, he won't want to do the next job you assign."

Hello, defeat. Next stop humiliation. "Fine. Here's your Binky, you overgrown infant." Cheeks warm, Roman fished the pacifier out of his backpack. Wally brightened with a joyful yowl and snatched the pacifier, scooting off to drop it on the ground and lick every centimeter of the pink plastic.

Emery gaped. "You're kidding. His reward is a baby pacifier?"

"Unfortunately. His previous owner said his son's kept going missing until he found Wally's stash under the sofa. All ten of them. He doesn't chew them for some reason so I don't worry he'll swallow the pieces, just licks and licks and gathers them like they're a brood of chicks and he's the mother hen. It's the weirdest dog behavior I've ever seen and if my siblings found out they'd never let me hear the end of it."

Emery exploded with a peal of giggles that had him laughing too. Her hair had come loose from the clip, swirling around her face in the unruly mass he remembered from long ago. He felt the desire to reach up and tuck a strand behind her ear.

Whoa. He stood and held out his palm to the dog. "All right, buddy. Bring it."

The dog curled his body tighter around his prize and turned his back to Roman.

"You're interrupting quality Binky time." Emery's cheeks were pink from laughter. She wiped her eyes.

"Wally, I said bring it."

The dog's head swiveled and it was another three seconds before Roman heard it too. A car. Hagerty rolled off the road toward their grassy hideaway and stopped. He got out.

"So you found it. Good work," he said. "I was nearby so I'd like to think I'd have tracked it down eventually."

Roman stood and snagged an anxious glance at Wally, but Emery somehow moved into position to block Hagerty's view of the dog and his toy. Had she done that on purpose, knowing Roman would be mortified if the cop found out?

They filled Hagerty in about the oar while he photographed the car from every angle. Opening the door with gloves, he videotaped the interior, removing her wallet and phone, which he bagged.

He heard Emery sigh and found himself empathizing. How long would it take before she got her wallet back? And with a baby to care for? He considered for the first time that she might be struggling to provide for her sudden charge. Paying for care while she did her job as a traveling nurse must cost a mint.

"We'll have to hang on to your vehicle for a bit," Hagerty said.

She gave one firm nod. Roman admired her strength. Always had.

Hagerty pocketed his phone. "I'll have the car towed and analyzed at the lab. Not going to lie. It'll take a couple of weeks at the minimum. At least you can start the insurance process, maybe get a rental."

Expensive. Her frown deepened.

Wally barked.

"What's the matter with him?"

A car appeared through the deep grass, bumping and jouncing.

The sunlight on the windows was blinding.

The tall grass bent in both directions as the car plowed right for them.

Emery snagged Wally's leash, uncertain. Sensations spun through her, the swish of the grass parting under the tires, a glint of glass, the flash of silver chrome. It seemed unreal that they might be crushed now, while she'd been focused on the quickest and cheapest way to get home to Ian.

The vehicle punched toward them like a metal fist.

Fear made her sluggish. Which way to run? She tried to dart to the side. *Too late.*

Roman dove at her, snagged her around the middle, hurtling the three of them to one side. They tumbled in a tangle of elbows, knees and paws. Wally yelped as he skidded onto his back, ungainly legs paddling the air. A millisecond later Hagerty dove onto the ground next to them. Through the fringe of grass she saw the car slam to a stop near the police cruiser. Wheels dug into the mud as the driver changed course, yanked the vehicle back toward the road. With a squeal of tires, it retreated.

Roman was on his feet, slipping on the damp ground as he scrambled.

Wally barked and leaped upright and though she tried to hold on to his leash, he yanked it clean out of her fingers and took off after Roman. She got up at the same time as Hagerty and they ran, following Roman's path through the wall of grass, up the slight slope to the road.

Her fuzziness morphed into fear. Roman and Wally would be no match for a murderous driver. Frantic breaths clawed their way out of her mouth and her heart rate soared.

Hagerty panted as he came to a stop. A moment later

she did too at the sight of Roman and Wally staring at the empty road in the direction the car had escaped.

Relief, both strange and comforting, flowed through her. No way they could have caught up. Silly to imagine Roman and Wally might have been in danger.

Roman swiped at the dirt on his forehead. "You okay, Emery?"

"Fine, now that my heart's started beating again. One minute we were talking and the next..." She breathed out, analyzing. "It seemed as though the driver was surprised to see a police car. Was that your take also?"

Roman nodded. "Whoever it was had to be responsible for your crash, or an accomplice, because they knew exactly where to look. It's not visible from the road."

"And the fact that they took off like a spooked horse," Hagerty added.

The most telling behavior of all. "Innocent people don't flee an accident scene?"

Hagerty reached for his handheld radio. "Correct."

Roman huffed out a breath. "I couldn't even get a partial plate number. You?"

Hagerty shook his head. "No, and my car camera won't have anything since it was facing the other way. Might have been a Mercedes, black paint."

She'd thought Mercedes too, but that was about as much as she'd been able to notice.

"Could be," Roman said. "By the time I caught up, they were nearly around the turn."

"What about that?" Emery pointed.

Hagerty looked at his body cam as if he'd forgotten about it. "Might have gotten a glimpse before I hit the dirt." He flicked a clump of soil off the lens.

"A glimpse could be enough." Roman brushed the dirt

from his clothes. "Can you forward the footage to Security Hounds?"

"No. That's property of the police."

Emery saw Roman's jaw firm, shoulders gone military straight as he prepared for battle.

"One look is all I'm asking. A screen shot is fine. You said yourself it will take weeks to go over Emery's car and now you've got an almost hit-and-run on your hands."

Was Roman pushing too hard? Finesse was not in his repertoire, at least from what she remembered.

And then he surprised her by shoving his hands in his pockets. "I'd really appreciate your help on this, Officer. Garrett would be the point person on this case and he's an ex-cop. He wouldn't ace you out."

Emery had to stop herself from staring.

Roman's unexpected humility did the trick.

"I guess maybe we could do that," Hagerty said.

Roman exhaled. "You have my word that if we find anything helpful, you will be our first call."

Hagerty sniffed. "We'd better be."

Roman took Wally's leash. They left Hagerty at his vehicle, talking into his radio. Wally scampered to the rutted mud and snagged his pacifier, grudgingly handing it over to Roman.

Back in Roman's Bronco, Emery tried to rub the grass marks from her pants. She'd always detested stains. They reminded her she'd worn her sister's hand-me-downs since she was six years old and their parents divorced. Their mom had moved to Europe, found a new way of life and a new man. Denise went through life skidding from one mess to the next, and Emery and her father had been the cleanup team. Until she'd had enough.

I'm not doing it, Dad. No more and you shouldn't either.

Diane is a grown woman and now she's shown up with a baby that she figures we should support. I can't do it. I won't do it. I've got my nursing career, my own apartment and I'm not coming to the rescue. Not this time.

I understand, honey. I really do. We'll talk soon.

But soon never came. If only she'd known what would happen barely two weeks later. Diane would move into Lincoln Taylor's guesthouse, insisting he was the father of her child. Lincoln allowed her to stay but refused a paternity test. More drama from which Emery was happy to be well out of. Diane called their dad with a rosy report of Lincoln's warming to his son. It seemed as though her sister might actually be putting things back together...until that strange text.

Emery tried to put the past from her mind. The present was messy enough. Her morning call to the hospital had indicated no improvement for her sister, and she hadn't been able to reach anyone who could update her on her father's condition.

Too much for me to handle, Lord.

But somehow she had to. Ian needed her. And God would help her deliver.

She snagged a sideways glance at Roman. "That was... nice the way you asked for Hagerty's cooperation."

He shrugged. "Learned a thing or two about dealing with people in the military. And like Theo used to say..." He trailed off and gripped the wheel, a vein in his jaw jumping.

She finished softly, "Patience wins over force."

He didn't look at her. *Done talking.* Never wanted to even think about all the love her father had showered on him. Her spirit filled with bitterness and anger.

"He would have chosen to believe in you, no matter what the facts said," she muttered.

His quick glance showed the mocha of his eyes had darkened. "I know you want to acknowledge only the best in him, Ree, but in my experience, facts win out every time."

Roman might have learned a bit about patience, but his flinty unforgiving nature hadn't softened one iota. He wouldn't extend any grace to her father. "You're not stuck on facts, you're hung up on the disappointment because of all the people that hurt you in your life. Your mother, Jax and my father." She saw him flinch as her arrow plunged deep. Shame licked at her but she shook it off. The silence thickened until it nearly swallowed her up. She forced some deep breaths and kept her thoughts to herself as they returned to the ranch.

SIX

Beth met them at the door. "Surprise visitor here to see you, Emery."

Her nerves prickled. Did she have the fortitude for any more surprises?

But a familiar cry had her running toward the living room.

Gino's ruddy face broke into a smile when he saw her, the light gleaming on his prematurely bald head encircled by a wispy fringe of hair. Ian was tucked against his chest. "There you are."

She hurried and wrapped them both in a hug before she took her nephew. "This is Gino Kavanaugh," she said by way of introduction, "and this is Ian." She savored the warm heft of the baby. "And how's my big boy?" Ian offered a gummy smile and grabbed for her hair. She twirled him until he gave up a belly laugh and she buzzed a raspberry onto his cheek. The lurch in her heart told her that despite her anger at her sister, love had found a way in. A chill rippled her spine. Love wasn't enough to keep him safe. What if he'd been in the back seat of her car the day before?

Thanks, God, for keeping Ian away from the danger.

Her mouth went dry as she realized her predicament. Now, Ian wasn't away. He was right here in Whisper Valley where she'd been nearly drowned, run over and stalked in her hotel room.

Cradling Ian to her shoulder, she allowed Beth to gesture them into chairs. Stephanie and Garrett joined in, their identical body types and coloring startling. Wally galumphed over to Emery and nosed the baby's socked foot, brows crinkling. "Gino and Diane went to school together. They've known each other since fifth grade. He's been a good friend, a lifesaver, in fact."

He shrugged and scratched at his sandy mustache. "Diane looked me up after Ian was born. Asked me to help and I said yes, of course. That's me, a yes man all the way, especially where Diane is concerned." He blushed. "Have a passel of nieces and nephews so I'm familiar with baby care. Diane and Ian lived with me for a few months before she decided to confront Lincoln." He bobbed his knee. "After Diane's accident, I figured I could help Emery with Ian since I work online. Doesn't matter where from, as long as there's a wireless connection. I rented a unit in Emery's complex and became good old Uncle Gino."

Emery smiled at him. "Without Gino, I don't know how I would have managed and that's the truth."

"How wonderful," Beth said. "A gift from God."

She wanted to agree wholeheartedly but her nerves were bow-taut. "But what are you doing here now?"

Gino shrugged. "I was worried. You called me from some number I didn't know, all you said was you'd had an accident. I called back repeatedly, but I couldn't get you."

"I called from the cell Roman loaned me." She'd told him her temporary location, but not many details.

She'd earned his recrimination, realizing she hadn't checked the messages on the cell Roman had given her. A seasoned mother would do better, not a mommy impersonator such as herself. Waves of guilt swept over her at her own negligence. "I'm sorry. Things have been…unsettled. I should have told you more in my message."

His glasses magnified his eyes in an owlish fashion. "What happened to you, Emery…" He darted a look around the room. "I mean, Emily?"

"It's okay, Gino. They know my real name. No keeping secrets from the Wolfes, since they've known me since I was a kid." She took a deep breath and told him in as succinct a manner as possible about her harrowing return to town.

His skin drained of color. "Who's after you?"

"That's what the cops are trying to figure out," Roman said. "How did you get to Whisper Valley, Gino?"

Roman's question startled her. Why was he asking?

Under the mustache, Gino's lip crimped. "I took the bus."

"Why?" she asked. "Didn't you want to drive?"

"My car wouldn't start and I was getting more and more worried. I packed up Ian in his car seat and got on the bus and then took a taxi from the station to here."

She patted Ian's back when he fussed. Beth was at her side in a moment, all the dogs watching. "Let me walk him. I should remember how to lull him. The twins were terrible sleepers."

"That was Garrett's fault," Stephanie said. "He kept me awake."

Garrett twirled a pencil. "Okay, I'll own that, but all the rest of the trouble we got into during our formative years is on your shoulders."

Stephanie's smile was impish. "Probably."

Gratefully Emery handed her the wriggling baby. Beth began to walk in gentle loops, bobbing him up and down and patting his diapered bottom. She limped a little, her jaw tight, but her smile was beatific.

Gino still fingered his mustache, nervous.

She didn't want to ask in front of the Wolfe family, but she forged ahead. "What aren't you telling me?"

His gaze darted around the room. After a long pause, he spoke. "Last week I had this feeling that someone was following me while I was out walking Ian."

She gasped. "Why didn't you tell me?"

"I was afraid it was paranoia. I've been an insurance investigator for twenty years so you get to be distrustful." He shot her an accusing glance. "Maybe I'm right to be paranoid. I mean, you're living with an alias, so…"

Roman leaned forward. "Did you see who it was following you? A man? Woman?"

Gino shook his head. "Might have been a rental. I noticed it when I stopped to adjust Ian's blanket. Then when I got coffee on our way back, I saw the same vehicle again outside the shop."

Garrett watched as his sister jotted notes on her iPad. They weren't on the case officially, but he was secretly happy to see her acting as if they were.

"Make? Model?" Stephanie asked. Beth listened intently as she continued to joggle Ian.

He shrugged. "Compact. Dark, four-door."

Roman frowned. "You didn't notice the license plate? A partial?"

Gino scowled. "No, I'm not a detective, clearly, just a nanny. My insurance duties are mostly online sleuthing. I'm not the Dick Tracy–type."

"It might be nothing." Emery saw the collective Wolfe family frowns. It wasn't nothing. It was terrifying, the world spinning uncertainly around her, clouded with danger. The question that was foremost in her mind every single morning since the shooting presented itself again.

What should I do? The question had assumed even more heft since she was now responsible for a child. Most often in these moments she descended toward panic until she remembered her father's "top-three" list.

If there's too much, Ree Ree, pick the top three things you have to do for that day. Three is easy, right?

First, go back home.

Care for Ian.

Book more nursing jobs to keep them afloat.

The rest…rent a car, continue to visit her sister and father, etc., etc. would all happen eventually.

"You should—" Roman started.

"No." Her temper snapped to life in that one tiny syllable. She tried to clamp down on the rising emotion. "I'm sorry, but do you know how often I've heard that from people in the last six months? Cops, lawyers, social workers, nurses have all said, you should do this or that…and then they vanish and it's me left do it all. I'm only one person." She cringed at the desperation ringing in her own words. *Deep breath, Emery.* "I know you mean well, all of you. I appreciate what you've done for me and I'll continue to cooperate with Hagerty as best I can, but I'm taking Ian home. Time for another bus ride, sweetie." She held out her hands for the baby, proud that they did not shake. There were no friends here in Whisper Valley. Only people who hated what her father had done, thought her sister a tramp, and the Wolfe family who pitied her. She didn't need that.

"Actually," Gino said. "Um, can I talk to you privately?"

Her gut clenched.

Beth laid her cheek on the top of Ian's head. "I'll greedily accept a few more minutes with this cutie. Who knows when I'll have a grandbaby to hold?"

Stephanie rolled her eyes.

"Don't look at me," Garrett said. "I just killed my last surviving houseplant."

With a feeling of dread, Emery followed Gino to the porch. She could feel the weight of Roman's gaze as she left.

"Whatever you're going to tell me is more bad news, isn't it?" she said the moment the door closed behind them.

"I really hate to give you this." He pulled an envelope from his pocket. "And you know I'm going to help you however I can."

The return address was a bank and the sticker on the envelope read *Forward* to her apartment address. The low-grade worry hitched into full-blown fear. "What is this, Gino?"

His lips puffed as he blew out a breath. "It's a letter of default for your father's cabin. It was forwarded to your apartment when you put in the request with the post office."

A request that she'd finally handled much later than she should have, but she blamed that on Ian's arrival and all the other bombs that had detonated after her father's arrest and her sister's injury.

"It showed up in your mailbox yesterday right after you left, along with these." He handed over several more. "I opened them. You told me to handle anything important anytime you were away nursing or whatever. The short story is the bank is foreclosing. Your dad hasn't been making payments on the place."

Foreclosing. Missing payments. "But…he's in jail. How could he possibly have been keeping up with his finances? I knew there was a payment due at the end of the month but…"

Gino looked at a spot over her head. "The problem didn't start with his incarceration. It seems he's been delinquent before, repeatedly. They sent a thirty-day notice last year and he managed to pay that and stave off action, but not this time." Finally his gaze traveled to her face. "I did some digging, used some channels I shouldn't have and, um, he'd taken out a second mortgage as well. To cover…expenses. Likely the same reason he worked as a handyman on this ranch, I think. His military pension wasn't enough to cover it."

Her heart plummeted to her shoes. *Expenses.* He'd helped pay for her nursing school and though she'd repaid every last nickel, it had taken her a year to do so. Had that contributed to his insolvency? And her sister's stint in a rehab facility had cost tens of thousands. Likely Diane hadn't come near to repaying it, if she'd even tried at all. Her father had bankrupted himself for them. Is that why he had told her to go home?

"I'm so sorry," Gino said.

Her heart boomed in her chest. "But there must be some way to stop it… If I repay…?" *With what?* She was barely surviving. Tears blurred the writing on the envelope. "A leniency schedule?"

He shook his head.

"So there's nothing I can do?" she whispered.

"The cabin is lost, I'm afraid. If I had the money, I'd pay it off in a flash."

"I know you would." Pulling in breaths through her nose, she tried to stave off hyperventilation. Her father would be crushed to lose his cabin *paradise* as he called Whisper Valley. He'd rather sell off all his possessions than let go of his home. Then again, what did she know of him, this man who refused even to see her when he'd been remanded to jail? That hurt most of all. Perhaps deep down he blamed her for giving up on Diane.

Gino put a hand on her forearm. "There's...not much time."

She blinked. "Time?"

He nodded. "The foreclosure begins a week from today."

One week? Of course. Why not? No sense prolonging the agony.

"Somebody will need to pack up his belongings," he added gently.

And that would fall to her too, of course. Along with a baby and everything else. Her head swam and she felt like screaming.

He offered a faint smile. "I brought my laptop along so I could stay and help you with packing and the baby. Like I said, have Wi-Fi, will travel." He sighed. "Sorry, not the time to joke."

"I couldn't ask for a better friend. I appreciate it." She barely managed the statement around the lump in her throat. She caught a flicker of emotion that he quickly concealed. "Is there something else?"

"No, nothing. I'll...go in and get Ian ready to drive to the cabin. Give you a minute, okay?" He patted her back. "I'm real sorry to have to tell you. Your dad would never have wanted you to deal with all this alone."

He let himself back inside.

A dark cloud ballooned in her stomach. Her top three had just changed. Again.

Care for Ian.

Pack up her father's belongings.

Maybe book a local nursing job to pay for a rental car back home at the end of the week.

She wondered how she'd explain to the Wolfes and

Roman that her father was a deadbeat in addition to a would-be murderer.

Roman wouldn't be surprised.

In those brown eyes, she'd see the self-righteous glint and the hurt underneath.

His thoughts were clear as a winter sky. *Never should have trusted him. He wasn't the man I thought he was.*

Despair weighed her down as she forced her feet back into the Wolfes' den.

Roman kept urging Wally out from underfoot as he hauled a bag of supplies his mother had packed to the Bronco.

He kept his jaws clamped shut to prevent him voicing to Emery the thoughts rocking his brain. *Your father bankrupted himself? And now that's your problem too?*

But Emery could barely get the words out and even a thick-skulled guy like himself could see she was near her breaking point as she climbed into his vehicle, strapping Ian into the car seat Gino had brought with him.

Beth stood in the doorway, face pained, having been unable to convince Emery to stay at the ranch. She waved and he saw her wince under the bright smile.

That tiny tell ratcheted his muscles. Beth desperately needed surgery for the back condition that caused her unending pain. She'd steadfastly refused the procedure due to the cost and length of recovery *until Security Hounds lands on all four paws*, as she put it.

His jaw clenched. They would be set, if the Cars for K-9s event went off as he'd planned it.

Their fledgling detective work was too sporadic and there wasn't a huge market for bloodhound pups so they'd curtailed their breeding program. They needed to snag a search and rescue contract with the county and he knew just the way to make that happen.

He drove to a quiet sloping road through the pine trees. Ian gurgled from the back seat and Gino played some sort of game with his toes. Emery stared grim-faced out the front window. Wally sat backward on the front seat between Roman and Emery, staring at the baby action going on in the rear, thumping Roman's shoulder with his eagerly wagging tail.

"Don't drool on the kid, Walls."

Gino chuckled. "I'm diverting the saliva slinging."

Roman wasn't sure how he felt about Gino. Something about the man plucked a distrustful chord, but Roman didn't trust much of anybody. Gino the friendly baby helper would have no reason to lie about his reasons for showing up. Would he? No use talking to Emery about it, or anything else. She was mute, every muscle strained.

He'd found some flattened cardboard boxes from their bulk shipment of dog food and rolls of packaging tape, the only way he could think to assist. His anger at Theo threatened to explode like the volcano that had erupted twelve thousand years before to form Crater Lake.

Theo had shot someone and gotten himself jailed, and he'd left a mess behind that was flowing over onto his daughter. He deserved nothing. Emery should leave town and let the bank send people to dump his belongings at the nearest auction house. The twenty miles of road did nothing to mellow his anger. They bumped along an uneven graveled path until they came to a wood-sided cabin with overgrown shrubs crowding the curtained front windows.

As soon as he put it in Park, she was out, striding to the door of the cabin as Gino extracted the baby. Wally hovered at Gino's side, his big nose sniffing at the wriggling bundle. "Hang onto him," Gino said, suddenly thrusting the baby at Roman. "I have to get the car seat loose. We'll have to rent a car at some point when we're done packing."

Startled, Roman gathered Ian close. Too close? Not close enough? It seemed like the baby's limbs were all wobbly and not working together. He'd never actually held a baby, he realized in that moment. Not a human one, only the newly born puppies he'd tended after he'd returned stateside. But dogs were born with eyes and ears sealed shut, balls of chubby helplessness. Ian craned his little head in Roman's direction, an old man's frown crinkling his feathery brows. Was Roman grabbing him too tightly? Loosening his grip could result in him dropping the tiny human who'd flung out a fist to bat at Roman's baseball cap.

"Whatcha need, baby boy?" *Baby boy.* The nickname he'd both loved and despised, bestowed on him by his uncle Jax. For a moment he could only stare into Ian's small perfect face, buffeted by the flood of memories.

I haven't stopped loving you, baby boy, but there's room in my life for a wife and more kids, Roman. You're gonna be seventeen soon. Can't you understand that?

There's no room in mine, he'd wanted to shout, his adolescent rage spilling into oaths, slammed doors, a hastily packed bag. *You replaced me, gave me up for someone else.*

Uncle Jax had tried to talk, repeatedly reaching out over the years, including a text only the week before Emery's attack at the river.

Hey, baby boy. Just thinking about you.

He hadn't replied, though he'd ached to. Every time he thought of Uncle Jax his heart was filled with a mixture of shame, sadness, disappointment and regret. He wasn't seventeen anymore, hadn't been for a decade, so why wouldn't he reach out to his uncle?

A bird hurtled from the thick trees with a raucous cry and Roman reflexively clutched Ian closer. The bird was probably startled by a fox or feral cat. Wally's nose quivered as he tracked the bird. Roman felt uneasy. Theo's cabin was remote, too far away from help if Emery needed it.

The late afternoon sun sank behind the distant hills. Wind rattled the branches. Gino was still wrestling with the car seat so Roman walked Ian to the cabin, whistling to Wally to follow. He found Emery inside, standing in the middle of a small living room on a braided rag rug. She was frowning at the lumpy sofa and the bookshelves crowded with detective fiction. There was a scent of pipe tobacco and Emery had already opened the small kitchen window to air it out. Theo and his pipe. The ache of it cycled through him, as he was sure it did with Emery.

Wally plowed in, awash in an avalanche of new scents to experience.

"I...uh... Here," he said, handing Emery the baby. "He feels like he might be cold, but I'm not sure how he's supposed to feel so..." His babbling dried up.

She gathered Ian close, much less awkwardly than he had, kissing him absentmindedly on the forehead and murmuring something he didn't catch. That tender tableau hitched his breathing.

What are you here for anyway, Roman? She doesn't enjoy your company and the feeling is mutual.

She surveyed the stuffed bookshelves and the kitchen with ancient cupboards no doubt crammed with things. Her sigh was weary, resigned. "This is going to take weeks."

"I'll help." Had he really said that? Now? With everything he had to do for the Cars for K-9s event? What would

Emery think if she knew he was a temporary partner with the Taylors?

He straightened. What was wrong with that? They were the victims, not the perpetrators.

She quirked a brow at him, probably trying to figure out how to decline his offer.

"I… I mean…"

Gino's arrival saved them both. "I'll put this in one of the bedrooms." There was a small insulated bag slung over his shoulder. "Brought along a few prepared bottles and his snacks, some diapers and clothes too."

Ian decided at that moment to cry. Wally jerked away from his sniffing and let out a blast of a bark, which made the baby cry louder. Roman quieted the canine. The dog settled into a low-grade whine as the baby continued to fuss.

"He needs a nap." Emery's exasperation was clear as she looked around.

Gino finally entered with the car seat. "We can put him down on your dad's bed until we get a porta crib. Watch him to be sure he doesn't roll off and roll up some towels as a bumper. Can you get me a clean diaper and I'll change him first?"

Emery pulled one from a bag Beth had provided.

Roman felt envious of their efficient partnership. He eyed the bookshelves, every inch crammed. "I'll fill some boxes."

Emery shoved the hair away from her face. "This is going to take weeks, especially with a baby."

Gino's mouth thinned. "We can do it. We've been handling everything for six months, just the two of us."

Roman cocked his chin. "That mean you can't tolerate a little assistance?"

"Not from someone who despises Theo."

He gaped. Not what he'd expected. He was rallying a response when Emery gestured to Gino. "Why don't you take Ian into the bedroom? Maybe he'll nap for you. You're the baby whisperer."

Gino didn't look at Roman as he accepted the whimpering child and left the room.

Emery turned and fished her credit card out of her pocket. At least Hagerty had been able to return it with her wallet. "I'm sorry to ask, but is there any way you could get us a portable crib?"

"It's not a great idea to stay up here alone after what happened to you."

"I don't have a choice. There's no one else to take care of my dad's belongings."

No one else to clean up the mess her father had left behind. No one to care for Ian but her and Gino. She should stay at the ranch. But he could not say the words because her lips were trembling and there was a sheen in her eyes of tears she did not want to shed, not in front of him.

He closed his mouth, gesturing away her credit card. "I know where I can borrow one." *She needs you to get a crib. She doesn't want your help.* Enough said. "I'll bring the boxes in before I go get it." He flipped the light switch, relieved that the power worked. At least that bill was paid up. For how long?

He'd nearly reached the porch when he heard an engine, a car winding along the lonely road. No other houses out this way and the road did not connect to any other major thoroughfares.

His stomach tightened.

Who would be driving to Theo's cabin? And why?

SEVEN

"A visitor. I'll see what they want, okay?" He hustled out with Wally in tow and closed the door behind him. His gut churned. Someone had learned she'd come to town? Ready to spew more hatred at her and her sister's child for what had happened?

It was a Mercedes, black. Three people got out. Innkeeper Hilary, her ex-husband, Lincoln, and his brother, Mason. Here? Why would they come to Theo's place? What could they want?

He managed a friendly smile. *They are your business partners, remember?*

Hilary zipped her sleek jacket and reached into the car for a cardboard box while Lincoln, dark-haired, lean and muscular, stared at the cabin. Mason took the box from Hilary. He was shorter than his brother, his frame stockier. When he stepped toward Roman, he subtly lurched, favoring one leg. They'd only spoken on the phone so Roman was unaware the damage from the bullet hadn't fully resolved. Would it be an injury that would impact him the rest of his life?

"Roman," Hilary said, surprised. "I didn't expect to see you here. We were planning on leaving this box on the porch since we didn't know where else to send it."

Wally stood on hind legs, front paws balanced against Roman's hip to sniff the carton as it passed into Roman's arms. "I was bringing up some packing boxes." He paused, figuring he had to add some sort of explanation. "Place is being sold."

Lincoln cocked his head. "Selling?" He raised a brow. "Nah. Not Theo. He seemed like the type that would live out in sticks until his last day. Let me guess. Foreclosure?"

Roman shrugged, feeling a swell of irritation. "Not my business." Nor Lincoln's.

Lincoln's expression was calculating. "Diane said he was struggling financially."

Roman hid his surprise that Diane had shared that fact with Lincoln but clearly not with Emery. Then again, there had been serious friction between the sisters.

Lincoln leaned against the car, arms folded over his muscled chest. A gym rat, obviously. He should try filling holes and running bloodhounds all day. Better than any workout.

Hilary shook her head. "That explains why she showed up insisting you support her and the baby. The daddy pipeline was drying up."

Lincoln frowned. "Maybe she was telling the truth about Ian. Maybe he is mine."

Hilary's expression was as cold as her words. "More likely she was lying. As you'd expect from someone who took up with a married man."

A dark flush crept up his neck. "We were having problems, Hilary. Divorcing, remember? We were waiting on lawyers."

She glared. "You never could wait for anything, could you?"

Roman would gladly have been anywhere else but in the middle of this family drama.

Mason shifted. "Uh, this doesn't seem like the right time to hash all this out. Lincoln can take a paternity test down the road if he wants to."

Lincoln shoved a hand through his hair. "I was considering it but I hadn't had time to make the decision when she…"

Hilary interrupted. "You made it clear you never wanted children, not when we were married. I don't see why you'd want one now."

"Think of how I felt. Diane and I were getting things worked out." Lincoln shook his head. "I come home from a drive to find Mason shot, Diane unconscious and her dad being arrested."

Hilary grimaced at him. "Yes, and her father intended to kill you, don't forget, and got your poor brother instead. It was astonishing that Mason didn't bleed to death."

"Right," Mason said. "Talk about being in the wrong place at the wrong time. I was reaching for the light switch and kablam—a shot comes out of nowhere and down I go."

Roman remembered Mason's account of the shooting. He'd been upstairs, heard a noise and walked to the balcony, where he'd been shot without even being able to identify who'd done it. He'd passed out, then roused to find medics treating his gunshot wound and cops swarming the house. If only he'd been able to provide an eyewitness account to clear things up.

What things? The case was open and shut, wasn't it?

Lincoln's gaze clouded. "I don't know why Diane would have told her father things were bad between us, or why he'd bring a gun to the house."

"You did decline the paternity test," Mason said. "Maybe it set him off."

"Yeah, but I wasn't done mulling it over. No cause for him to become violent like that."

Hilary sniffed. "You should consider yourself fortunate. *You* didn't get hurt." She patted Mason. "Theo probably saved you from a woman trying to use her baby to trick you into a marriage, Lincoln."

"Please, you two," Mason said. "When Diane recovers..." His words trailed off.

If she recovers...

Mason held up his hands. "Anyway, sorry for airing out the family laundry. Dad's rolling over in his grave, no doubt. He'd talk your ear off about cars, but never personal stuff."

Lincoln's cheeks flushed and he didn't meet his brother's eye. "Right. Roman has things to do and so do we, so let's leave him to it."

Roman nodded. "Yeah. I need to get these inside."

Mason quirked a brow. "I'm surprised you'd be packing up Theo's place. Didn't know you had a connection to the Duncan family."

He shifted, reluctant to share but unwilling to lie. "Theo Duncan was a friend for a while." Before Hilary could ask the question that appeared to be forming, he added, "What's in this box?"

"Baby stuff. Diane left them at Lincoln's house." Hilary shrugged. "Outfits and some toys and bottles."

"How is she?" Lincoln said. "Diane, I mean."

"I don't know details. Still hospitalized," Roman said.

"What a tragedy," Mason said. "Hopefully not for too much longer."

"Why do you care?" Hilary demanded. "She and her father are the reason you're in pain and walking with a limp now."

Mason sighed. "Come on, Hil. Diane's father's in jail.
And hasn't she been punished enough? She's got a baby
and all, and honestly she was a good mother, from what I
could see. That's why we brought these things back here."
He pointed to the box in Roman's arms and caressed Wally
with his free palm. Wally snuffled at him. "Didn't seem
right to donate them. Figured maybe someone would come
and pick them up and deliver them to Emery. We saw her
in court that one time. We figured she'd get temporary custody, at least. Is that what happened?"

Roman took a breath. How much of Emery's business
was it all right to share?

He was saved from answering when the door opened
and Emery stepped out. The look of shock on the faces of
the three visitors was textbook.

Hilary gaped. "Wait a minute. Now I recognize you. You
look like your sister, even with the change of hair color."

Emery wrapped her arms around her middle. "Yes," she
said after a moment's hesitation.

"You might have used your real name when you checked
into my inn."

Emery stared at Hilary. "Would you, if you were me?
After everything that happened in this town?"

Hilary didn't answer.

"They brought some of the baby's things," Roman said.

Emery's posture was rigid with discomfort. "Thank
you."

"How's... I mean, how is he? The baby?" Lincoln asked.

Emery cocked her head. "I'm not sure why you'd want
to know, since you refused a paternity test, from what Dad
told me."

Hilary's eyes narrowed. "We're talking about the same
dad that shot Mason, right? Champion father material."

Emery's cheeks flamed. Roman put a hand on her forearm. This was turning into a disaster.

Lincoln was already edging back toward the car. "Okay. We'll be at the ranch to talk details tomorrow, Roman. The weekend is coming fast."

Emery shot him a look.

He felt his cheeks burn. "Yes. I'll be at the ranch at ten. We'll go over the info."

Mason smiled. "This is going to be the most amazing event ever to hit Whisper Valley. It's our chance to shine. Right, Lincoln?"

Lincoln acknowledged the remark with a shrug. Mason's smile dimmed. Hilary touched his arm. "Your brother's excited too but overwhelmed. Don't worry. He'll be at his best when the clients arrive." She turned to Roman, ignoring Emery completely. "We'll be ready. There's a lot riding on it."

Didn't he know it. Roman called Wally away from sniffing Lincoln's Mercedes.

After a deep breath, he walked inside behind Emery, sliding the box onto the table.

She jerked the window closed, locked it and pulled the curtains. "That was awkward, but inevitable, I suppose. I was bound to run into them in town. I guess the cat's out of the bag now. I won't need my alias. Emery Duncan, the youngest of the no-good family, has come back to Whisper Valley."

"Most folks won't think that."

She shook her head. "It's exactly what they'll think." After a beat, she added, "So you're partnering with the Taylor family? What's that about?"

"I should have said something sooner." He told her about the car show, wondering if he sounded defensive. Why

should he? "I'm hoping to land a contract with the local police departments and county to provide tracking services to
supplement our detective work," he explained. The idea had
been born out of a missing persons case with which they'd
assisted. Stephanie and Cleo had tracked a child who'd wandered away in a storm. The child's parents donated a small
sum to Security Hounds and begged the police department
to bring on a bloodhound instead of having to call for one.
"After many conversations with Hagerty, myself and the
police department, I worked up a plan with the Taylors for
a Cars for K-9s benefit. The dogs will be on site for some
demonstrations to wow the crowd."

"A win-win situation for both parties." Her posture was
stiff.

"The Taylors are donating ten percent of their take. If
the event brings in enough money, the county will offer a
contract with an agency for search and rescue."

"Security Hounds, of course?"

"We'd be the perfect choice. No other bloodhound training facilities around. I can prove their abilities with the
demonstrations we've planned for the weekend event at
the Taylor estate."

His mind latched on to all the small details that needed
to be tended to before the first Cars for K-9s event kicked
off at the ranch. It would be followed by a second demonstration on Sunday culminating in a reception at the Taylor showroom. Plenty of audience participation. Roman
intended for Security Hounds to have a presence in every
aspect. It had to work, since he'd blown up the budget with
advertising, revamping the dogs' travel trailer and even
gotten the family matching shirts and caps, much to their
dismay.

"We're going to be the group law enforcement looks

for when there's a fugitive, a lost child or pet, et cetera," he'd told them.

Steph was on board and Garrett was amenable, but Chase had doubts about extending themselves in what would be a 24/7, 365 day a year availability. Kara remained quiet, as per usual.

"We can't be all things to all people. Detectives, dog rescuers, et cetera," Chase had said.

"Steph, Garrett and I can handle the search and rescue aspect and we'll come together when there's a case that requires it," he'd insisted. "You and Kara can be floaters to pitch in whenever you can."

The project was in limbo until Beth stepped in. "I say we go for it, but without the county's buy in, we'll be dead in the water before we even start."

Dead in the water... Roman realized he'd been lost in his own jumbled thoughts as Emery watched him quietly.

"I'm going to get the contract." He was sure the Cars for K-9s weekend would seal the deal.

She cocked her head, the hair softly framing her cheek. "You're determined to help Security Hounds succeed."

He shrugged. "They're my family and Beth won't get the surgery she needs on her back until we clinch the business."

He'd braced for Emery to be upset at his participation with the Taylors, especially after Hilary's remarks. Instead she leaned her head against the wall, weariness etched in every shadow that played across her face.

"I'm glad you have family around you, Roman." Her voice was soft. "You deserve that."

Deserve? To be loved like he was by people who'd chosen him? He didn't believe that yet, which is why he was working so hard on the K-9 event. He was going to show them he was worthy.

She sighed. "But there's something wrong with the Taylors. I don't exactly know what. For all her faults, Diane wouldn't have gone to the house with murder on her mind and my father wouldn't have taken the blame or shot anyone himself unless he felt there was no other choice."

"I know you want to believe that. I did too."

She blinked. "You stopped believing pretty quick, didn't you? And you walked away."

From Theo…and from her.

The blanket of quiet was smothering.

"I'll get you that crib." He dug his keys from his pocket. As he called to Wally and pushed open the door, he noticed Gino in the bedroom patting Ian's back. He'd obviously been eavesdropping.

Gino darted a look at him just before he closed the door.

If he were still in the Navy, it'd make him take a good long look at Gino and earn the man an up close and personal examination from a nosy dog.

One thing was for certain.

Gino had secrets.

After an hour of the baby's screaming that left her nerves ragged, Ian finally fell asleep in his car seat with Emery curled up next to him on the floor. Eventually, she must have slept as well because her eyes flew open again a few minutes after eight o'clock. Her neck was beyond kinked, body outraged at having been sprawled on the hardwood.

Groggy, she got to her knees. The room was dark save for the small side table lamp and the light coming from underneath the closed door of the second bedroom, which Gino had claimed. She shoved her hair out of her eyes. No need to keep it dyed dark anymore, since her secret was out. Everyone knew she was in town and that made her feel naked, vulnerable. No doubt it was a mistake to stay in her father's cabin, but there seemed no other choice, no one else to tackle the packing. *All on you, Emery.*

Roman hadn't returned with the crib. She probably shouldn't have asked him about it anyway. It rankled her that he was business partners with the Taylors. They might not be criminals, but they surely wanted her father imprisoned for the rest of his life and they had strong opinions about her sister's motives.

So had she. In fact, she'd been convinced Diane's latest appearance in her mommy role was another way to take advantage of her father's good graces, one more mess she expected the family to clean up. Her own guilt left a sour taste in her mouth. Ian twitched in his sleep.

Not a mess. A child. She heaved out a breath and offered a prayer for God to soften her bitter heart.

...honestly she was a good mother, Mason had said.

The sentiment touched her, from a man who had no reason to say one nice word about any Duncan family member. For all her faults, Diane didn't deserve to be comatose with an unwilling sister raising her baby. "Lord, help me do my best."

Ignoring her protesting muscles, she took a knee next to her sleeping nephew. Ian's mouth puckered and she hastily tucked the blanket more snugly around him and rocked the seat until he quieted. As he settled once more, her gaze drifted to the clutter closing in around her, every item in need of packing away and disposing. Books, navy memorabilia, fishing lures, her father's beloved houseplants, now mostly dead after months of not being watered... The magnitude of the job flattened her until she forced a deep breath.

"Not impossible," she told herself with more cheer than

she believed. "With Gino's help, I can knock this out in a few days if Ian will cooperate." Then she remembered the basement and the groan made its way past her defenses. How much had her father accumulated since she'd last been down in that dank space?

She shot a look toward the bedroom. Gino had earned a few hours of rest, especially after his marathon bus trip with an infant in tow. She'd allow herself a quick peek while Ian slept. The front door was secured only by the worn bolt. It was something anyway.

The basement door opened and a rush of cool air bathed her face. She moved Ian away from the draft. "Be right back. I'll be able to hear you if you cry, okay?" Did other parents engage in one-sided conversation with their children?

She flipped the switch at the top of the stairs, which activated a bare bulb, a meager forty watts, but enough for her to use the stairs safely. She knew there were small windows set high in one of the basement walls, which would make the daytime packing easier. Tonight was simply recon, as Roman would say.

Dismissing him firmly from her mind, she decided on her "top three" for the rest of the evening. First, no matter how daunting, she'd scope out the contents of the basement. Second, compile a list of supplies necessary for the three of them to survive the packing phase. That would entail a trip into town, which made her insides quiver. All the haters were stoking their anger, no doubt. Third, call in to her agency and let them know she was unavailable for a few days. *Unavailable and unpaid*, she thought grimly. How long would her money hold out with the majority of it going toward her apartment rent?

One cement wall was floor-to-ceiling with rickety wood

shelves holding a hodgepodge of materials. Her father the pack rat...

Against the far wall was a metal desk, tidy, at odds with the rest of the space. On top was an iPad. Odd since her dad was a dinosaur where technology was concerned. Next to it was her father's favorite "Daddy's sweeties" mug, emblazoned with a photo of her and Diane. It was the last school photo before their mother and father divorced.

Marjorie Duncan was now Marjorie Watkin, her second marriage since she'd divorced Theo. She was aware of the situation with her daughter and ex-husband, of course. She'd even visited Diane in the hospital once, but she was the manager of a struggling travel agency. With nothing good to say about Theo Duncan, she'd managed a half-hearted offer.

I could, um, send some money when things pick up again. Or you could move to Virginia and maybe I could help with the baby when I'm not working.

Marjorie Duncan wanted nothing to do with raising a baby or resuming her position with a family she'd left two decades before. Emery appreciated the offer for what it was, polite and insincere. Mom didn't know her daughters anymore, didn't want to revisit any connection with their father and couldn't board the plane back to Virginia fast enough.

Just you, Ree Ree. With tears in her eyes, she moved closer to the desk and attempted to turn on the iPad. Dead. Naturally.

She picked up the mug and caressed it, her fingertip finding the chip. A sound made her clutch it to her chest. The baby? She was three steps toward the stairs when she heard it again. Slowly she swiveled around.

Wrong direction.

The sound was coming from outside. She stared at the

small windows. Shifting shadows stretched and undulated outside, wind-driven tree branches caught in the moonlight.

Branches, she decided. *You're in the forest, remember?* Acres of wild Siskiyou County, stretching halfway to Klamath Falls. She was reaching to return the mug to the desk when a shadow took terrifying shape against the moisture-speckled glass. Something white against the pane.

A hand, cupped, pressed to the window, the gleam of two eyes peering in.

With a scream, she dropped the mug and ran up the stairs two at a time, snatching Ian out of the car seat, startling him into a shriek. *Get out or stay in? If someone was out there...*

"Gino," she yelled. She ran to his bedroom. Empty. So was the bathroom. Where had he gone? Panicked, she fled into her bedroom, locked the door and then pulled out her phone, dialing without thinking.

Roman answered on the first ring.

"Roman, there's someone outside."

"Where are you?"

"Locked in the bedroom with Ian."

"I'm five minutes out. Make that three. Stay on the line with me."

She heard the revving engine, imagining she could detect Wally's slobbery panting in the passenger seat. Trying hard to both quiet the baby and her own breathing, she strained to hear any sounds from outside. Were those normal shadows writhing outside the curtains or someone approaching? It was as though she were being tossed in the river all over again, helpless, drowning... Roman's voice on the phone snapped her back to the present.

"Are you hurt? Ian? Where's Gino?"

"We're okay. I don't know where Gino is. Ian's crying

because I woke him up. I was in the basement and…" She froze as a human silhouette glided across the closed bedroom curtains. "Roman," she whispered over her thundering heart. "I think there's someone walking outside."

"I'm almost there. Hold on." In moments she heard his boots pounding over the gravel, a crash as the front door was kicked open, the scrabbling of dog nails on the hardwood.

"Emery," Roman said. "It's me. Stay in there while I check."

With a surge of blissful relief, she tried to calm herself and Ian, patting his bottom. "Shh, baby. Help is here."

Time passed with painful slowness until Roman's tap startled her.

"House is clear. You can unlock the door."

She did, with trembling hands, stepping out and, without any conscious intention, delivering herself into his arms. He embraced her and the baby, wrapping them close while Wally gave them an interested sniff before allowing himself free rein to explore the house.

She pressed her cheek to the rough fabric of Roman's flannel shirt. "I'm sorry for calling you," she whispered.

His embrace tightened. "Nothing to be sorry about. I was on my way here, anyway. Your call just lit a fire."

She realized she was snuggled against him, inhaling the enticing aroma of pine from his shirt. What's more, she was dismayed to find she was savoring the sensations. Quickly she straightened, shuffling the baby on her hip as he started crying again. "Um, my screaming woke him up. He's grumpy, for sure."

Roman cocked a look at her. "Found a trespasser, by the way."

"Who?"

He jerked a thumb behind him. Gino stood with his hands in his pockets. He wore a dark windbreaker and a baseball cap. His cheeks were flushed.

"I thought you were sleeping in the bedroom. Why didn't you come when I screamed?"

"I was outside. I didn't hear you. Is something wrong?"

She gaped. "Why in the world were you out in the cold?"

He shrugged. "I couldn't sleep. When I came out of the bedroom, you were dozing next to Ian so I figured I'd take a quick walk to loosen up. I went out the back door so I wouldn't let in a draft on you and Ian."

Roman was examining Gino's expression with the same intensity she saw in him when he'd been tracking with Wally. "She was almost drowned recently, stalked at the inn, and you left her here alone with a baby? Went for an evening stroll?"

Gino's flush deepened to scarlet. "I was no more than five minutes away tops, on the trail. I could have run back if I'd heard…"

"But you didn't hear," he snapped. "She screamed and you didn't head back until you saw my Bronco roll up."

His brows knitted. "The wind was blowing. I shouldn't have left, but I was desperate for fresh air." He turned to Emery. "I'm sorry. Are you two okay? Why did you scream?"

"I saw… I thought I saw…" She took a breath. "I was in the basement and I thought I saw a face at the window, looking in."

Gino's crimson cheeks paled to white. "Who?"

Emery shook her head and continued to joggle the baby. "I don't know. Roman, was there any sign of someone out there?"

"Not that I could tell. It's heavy grass so no prints would show, anyway. Wally wanted to drag me into the shrubs, but he was after a racoon or possum, likely."

She took in the two men staring back at her. They didn't believe she'd seen someone. She wasn't sure she believed herself. Had it been a human face at the window or the play of light and branches against the glass?

"I'm sorry. Probably my imagination. I guess I'm jumpy."

"You were almost murdered. Makes sense." Roman's tone was guarded and she couldn't decipher his expression as he strode toward the door. "I'll bring in the crib." He paused and tossed over his shoulder, "And I can stay the night on the sofa, me and Walls."

He didn't wait for her to reply before he headed outside.

Stay the night? She handed the baby to Gino. "Be right back."

She caught up with Roman at the Bronco where he hauled out a neatly folded portable crib. Rain drops spat at her.

"This was up in the attic at the ranch," Roman said. "Chase asked me to store it. He… Well he cared for his girlfriend's baby for a while. A painful breakup. Long story. Anyway, I know he wouldn't mind you using it for Ian."

"Roman, thank you for this and everything, but there's no reason for you and Wally to stay here."

His eyes sought hers. "Yes, there is."

"I was probably mistaken."

Roman stayed silent.

"And Gino's here with me. I know you don't trust him, but I do and I know him better than you." She paused. "My dad did, also."

Roman's frown deepened. "Maybe not a trustworthy character reference."

She bristled. "I'll make my own decisions about whom to trust."

Again, a long silence grew between them along with her kindling ire. She knew her father's heart and Roman had too, but he'd convinced himself he'd been betrayed. Did he see that whatever had happened that terrible night did not erase the goodness in her father's soul?

"Don't stay," she repeated. "We're fine."

"I busted your door lock."

"I'll put a chair under the knob for tonight."

He grimaced and started to reply, then stopped and sighed. "I'll come tomorrow to fix the lock."

She wasn't going to talk him out of that, she could tell. "All right. I'll pay for the materials. Just let me know how much." She turned to go but he grasped her hand.

"What if Gino is lying?"

She grabbed the crib and backed up a step. "As I said, I know Gino better than you do, like I know my father." What was she doing? Baiting him? Poking him toward a fight because that was easier than acknowledging the strange attraction she'd felt earlier? "I appreciate your help. Thanks for the boxes, and bringing the crib, and..." And holding her while she trembled in fear. She tipped her chin up.

She'd made her decision. She might be attracted to Roman, like she'd always been, but that was surface-level only. He was a bitter person who cast everyone outside the walls he'd built. There was no room for forgiveness or even space to entertain the possibility that her father was acting to protect his children. She didn't want him around to remind her how Theo Duncan had failed. The task in front of her was enough to do that.

"Good night, Roman."

She didn't stay to hear his reply as she carried the crib inside and closed the door behind her.

EIGHT

Roman knew he was overstepping, yet he simply couldn't divert his mind from Emery and the baby. Gino wasn't trustworthy. He knew it. He felt it. But it was her choice so he shouldn't interfere. Deep in his soul he was certain the person who'd tried to drown Emery was the same one who'd been lurking at the inn and Theo's cabin.

After a night of wrestling with the covers, he finally landed on something he could do. He'd provide her some independence in the form of a vehicle, a safe way out if things went bad. He'd called her cell at the ungracious hour of 6:00 a.m. She'd answered on the second ring and agreed after some intense convincing on his part. When he pulled up at the cabin at a little after seven o'clock with Wally sprawled in the back seat, she was standing on the porch, dressed in a windbreaker and jeans.

"Not bringing Ian?" He was surprised at his own disappointment. Things would be much less complicated without a baby along, but still...

"Gino's up. With the rain threatening, it's better not to take Ian out since he's had the sniffles." She held up a palm. "Gino loves Ian as much as I do and I trust him implicitly."

No matter what you say, he finished in his head. He shrugged. "Would have been nice, is all."

She shot him a sidelong glance under those impossibly thick lashes. "You're disappointed?"

"Wally is. He wanted to frisk Ian for any loose pacifiers."

Her laugh encouraged his and the tension between them melted. She turned to scrub Wally behind his pendulous ears. "Wally, you are a national treasure. They should put you on a dollar bill."

"He seems to think so."

She straightened and tucked the hair off her face. "I really appreciate the car. I want you to know I'm going to pay you back for all of this, the gas, the crib, everything."

"Nothing to pay back. The crib is a loaner and so is the car. Wait until you see it. It's no great shakes and it smells of dog but Steph hasn't gotten around to selling it. It's just had a rear fender replaced so it's in the shop in town."

"Still, gas and…"

He reached for her hand and squeezed. Her fingers were warm, strong. "No need."

When she answered, her voice was low. "I don't want you to do things because you feel guilt or pity for me."

He twisted toward her, startled. "That's not what I feel."

She cocked a look at him. "Really?"

He didn't know how to reply. His emotions were zinging around like kernels in a popcorn popper, but guilt and pity were definitely not in the bunch.

"We can clear out the elephant in the room, Roman. When you look at me, you see my father's betrayal. It hurts. You don't want anything to do with the Duncans so you must be helping me because you feel sorry for me and Ian."

"It's not like that."

"Yes, it is. Has to be, even though most everyone else won't come near us for any reason." She groaned. "That's the worst thing about it all, really, is the way people have stepped away, like they're afraid of catching something or ruining their reputations by sticking around."

Was she saying he'd done that? He'd stepped away, for sure, but she'd welcomed it. His actions had nothing to do with her anyway. A sizzle of regret lashed him. Whatever the reason, he had indeed sidestepped as far as he could from Theo, and by default, Emery. "I should have explained earlier. I… I mean, my behavior back then had nothing to do with you or worrying about what people might think or anything like that. Your father pretended to be something he wasn't, told me stories about honor and righteousness and self-control when he had none of those things. I don't keep people in my life who betray me."

She shook her head, lips pressed together. "I still believe my dad didn't do what he confessed to, but you know what, Roman?" Her eyes glittered like the crystalline waters of Crater Lake. "This might rock your world but I'd love him every bit as much if he was guilty."

He blinked in disbelief. "You'd love him if he'd planned a murder?"

Her chin went up, the answer short and pained. "Yes."

Attempted murder from a person who'd spouted on about love and God and the way to be a proper man? Acid and anger churned the coffee in his stomach. How had the conversation taken such a turn in the span of a few minutes? "It's not like we're talking about unpaid parking tickets."

She was silent, staring out the window for several beats before she answered. "Love doesn't turn on and off like that. It doesn't with God and it shouldn't with us. If he's really guilty, would I be crushed? Ruined in my heart? Of course. It would split open my soul." Her voice wobbled. "I'd never get over it but I wouldn't stop loving him." She swiped at a tear in the corner of her eye.

His heart lurched as he tried to take it in. He reached for her hand again, kissed the knuckles, desperate to ease her pain. "I'm sorry to make you cry. You... I mean, it's okay however you feel about it. I guess we're just two really opposite types of people."

She pulled a tissue from her pocket and wiped her face. "Not so different. You still love your uncle Jax."

The words took his breath away. He gripped the wheel. "Yeah, sure, but that's a completely different situation." Uncle Jax hadn't planned to kill anybody.

"So you've forgiven him? You still love him even though you believe he betrayed you?"

Forgiven Uncle Jax? He wasn't sure. Loved him? That was easier. He squirmed. Why did they need to talk about his uncle, anyway? "I've grown up some. I was young and insecure back then. I shouldn't have behaved the way I did."

"That's not an answer to the question."

He didn't like the question, or the whole conversation for that matter. He had to force himself not to exceed the speed limit as they took the winding road into town. This wasn't about him, though she was bent on making it such. He knew most of the fault for the debacle with Uncle Jax was his own stubborn adolescent behavior. He'd let it go, mostly. So why hadn't he ever returned Uncle Jax's calls? Talked to the man in the decade since the day he'd run away? Because Roman had found a new family to love him in the Wolfes? *A new family...* His own angry words rang in his memory as if he'd shouted them only moments before.

You found a shiny new family, Uncle Jax, with kids that are better than me, right? Jax's decision had uprooted Roman's worst fear, deeper than abandonment or pain or failure, the deep down, bone-shivering worry that he was not lovable.

He jumped when he felt her fingertips on his arm. "I'm sorry, Roman. What am I doing? I'm dumping on you. I shouldn't have brought up Uncle Jax."

"No big deal," he said, straightening slightly until she removed her hand.

"Yes, it is." She sighed. "I love my dad and if he did plan to shoot someone, I'll have to come to terms with that. But loving and accepting are two different things. My dad was generous and kind to you. He's still that man somewhere deep inside, no matter what happened. Can you allow for that possibility?"

It was too much. His delay in replying made her twist away from him to look out the window. Her profile was so lovely that he thought the rising sun could not compete. A shiver raced along his nerves. If things had been different, if he hadn't enlisted, gone away…if Theo hadn't done what he did…

No sense contemplating what might have been.

Wally's tail thwacked the rear seat as they arrived. The morning traffic consisted of several trucks cruising the main drag, their drivers in search of coffee or fueling their vehicles at the corner gas station with an attached auto repair place. The mom-and-pop grocery store was opening up for the day. "Got another fifteen before we can pick up the car. Need supplies?"

She huffed out a breath. "As a matter of fact, yes. I made a list."

He laughed. "Ever the organizer."

"That trait has come in handy when I was suddenly in charge of Ian. I went from taking care of myself to raising a helpless miniature human."

"I can't imagine. No other family members to step in and share the load?"

She shrugged. "Not really anyone suitable. My mother made a halfhearted effort but that wouldn't have worked out. He would have gone into foster care."

Like Roman had. The magnitude of her choice to take in Ian swept over him.

"You're doing great with him. He's blessed to have you." Blessed, completely.

She cocked her head in surprise. "Thank you. It's the hardest thing I've ever done."

And would continue to do until Diane recovered, if she ever did. What kind of courage did that take? To leap into another person's life for a season, or maybe forever. Like Uncle Jax had done. Again, his thoughts circled back to the past, his own mistakes.

He drove to the grocery store, jaw set. When he parked, Wally emitted a howl when Roman told him to stay put.

"Last time you knocked over the entire mac and cheese endcap along with the store manager. Your face is on a wanted poster in there."

Wally slammed a front paw into the seat for emphasis.

"You don't get what you want by throwing a fit. Stay."

Roman had a feeling Emery was holding back laughter as they hurried into the store.

She moved quickly, snagging things and tossing them into a handbasket. A stocky man with a barn jacket glanced at her from the bread aisle. Roman recognized him as he turned down their row, gaze still locked on Emery. Before he could say anything, she squared off with him.

"Can I help you with something?" she said to the staring man.

"You just look familiar, like someone who used to live here."

He started to intervene, but Emery spoke up.

"I am someone who used to live here."

The man's eyes narrowed. "I know you. Heard you were back. You're a Duncan."

The Taylors must have been talking. "Yes."

Roman put a hand on her arm. "This is Kevin. He's a mechanic here in town. Works on the Taylors' cars too."

Kevin nodded. "Yeah. And it was a real tragedy what happened to Mason. Guy probably won't ever recover fully." The rest was unsaid. *Because of your father.*

He felt the muscles in her shoulders tense and he eased in front of her. "Kev, Emery has nothing to do with that."

Kevin twirled a bag of bread. "You told everyone it wasn't Daddy's fault. Now where's Daddy? In jail, where he belongs."

"That's enough." Roman moved until he was inches from Kevin's chest, his own fury hot in his veins. "How about you behave like a civilized person? Not the place or time to air your opinions to a lady who's here to get groceries like you are. Is this how we treat people in Whisper Valley? That's the kind of man you are?"

Kevin looked up at Roman, who glowered down at him. The seconds ticked by as Roman considered whether he should escort Kevin out of the store or remove Emery from the situation. Either way, she wasn't going to be insulted anymore.

"Whatever." Kevin yanked himself around and shuffled to the checkout stand.

Emery sniffed and he realized she was fighting to keep from crying. He turned her toward him and embraced her. "Don't let him get to you. He's a hothead."

She leaned in and turned her face to his neck.

"No need to stay," he said, his lips grazing her cheek. "We can get supplies later."

She straightened. "No. No one is going to prevent me from getting Ian what he needs."

His breath caught as she straightened her spine, tipped her chin and blinked back tears. She strode toward the baby aisle and he scurried to catch up. In a few moments she'd grabbed a dozen or so items, including a large package of diapers, formula and some fruits, applesauce and bread. Jars of baby food and a pacifier completed the collection.

He was grabbing for his wallet when she produced hers with a dazzling smile. "Got mine back, remember?"

He knew better than to offer to pay, anyway.

After checking in with the mechanic, Emery was installed in the loaner Toyota. She was still obviously upset from the grocery store encounter but determined to put it behind her. The rain had begun to fall, swirling the tangle of trees that bordered the garage parking lot. He checked the wiper blades and gave her a thumbs-up as Wally scanned the cracked asphalt. She rolled down the driver's side window. "I promise I'll return it with a full tank of gas."

Desperation tightened his stomach. She was ready to go and he wasn't sure when he'd see her again. He'd told himself he was concerned for her safety, angry townsfolk now added to the list of dangers, but it went deeper. "Cup of coffee before you head on back?" He pointed to the small café across the street.

Her gaze was mournful. "As tempting as that sounds, I'd better scoot. Ian's been fussy lately and it's not fair to Gino to leave him for too long."

The door of the coffee shop opened and Mason Taylor came out, sipping from a cardboard cup, a cane in his free hand. He noticed them and saluted with his drink.

Emery's smile flickered, but she waved back. It had to be weird to see the guy her father had shot. Bad enough when they'd appeared at the cabin. Mason would be heading to the ranch for their morning meeting, which was also probably strange to Emery. The Taylors were prospering in a town where she was greeted with animosity and anger.

Wally's head whipped toward the trees.

Roman tensed. "What's up, boy?"

Wally woofed, a long low sound, a moment before a rock came hurtling through the air.

Emery screamed as something crashed against the glass. Roman and Wally immediately sprinted off toward the trees. She stared around wildly, noting the chip out of the rear window and a rock rolling away until it came to rest a few feet from a sprawl of weeds. A rock…hurled at her car?

In the distance she saw that Mason had dropped his coffee and was sprinting over.

"Emery…" he called out. Before he reached her, he tripped on an uneven spot with his damaged leg and sprawled face-first on the pavement, his cane clattering next to him.

She flung open the door and scrambled over to him. He'd tucked his knees and awkwardly made it to a sitting position before she reached him.

She retrieved his cane.

With her help, he got to his feet and looked ruefully at a smear of mud on his pants. "Great."

The shop owner burst through the door, scanning from Emery to Mason. "Should I call an ambulance?"

Mason waved him off. "Not for me. How about you, Emery? I heard you scream and I came running, or tried to anyway."

"Somebody threw a rock at the car, but I'm completely fine. Are you sure you're okay?"

Mason rubbed his knee. "Just bruised, I think."

Roman returned, breathing hard. Wally's tail wagged as if he'd just had a wonderful exercise, his pink tongue lolling.

"Whoever it was is long gone," Roman said through gritted teeth.

Mason eyed Wally. "He couldn't track him down?"

"Not without a scent to target and I didn't think to take the rock. Wally thought it was a great game of some sort, especially when the squirrel made an appearance." Roman took a photo before he picked up the rock with his fingers covered by his coat and offered it to the dog. Wally took great sniffs of it and sat in a heap, drool ribboning from his mouth.

"Possibly he was wearing gloves, or Wally doesn't feel like tracking anyone since he just had a full-out sprint." Roman was irritated but Emery didn't blame the dog. She'd hardly had time to realize what had happened either.

Roman grabbed a plastic bag from the Bronco and dropped the rock in.

Mason frowned. "Why would someone throw something at Emery's car?"

Emery hugged herself against the chill wind. "Word's gotten out that I'm not Emily Bancroft. My family and I aren't the most popular people in town. A mechanic by the name of Kevin told me as much in the grocery store."

"Our Kevin? Why...?" Mason trailed off. "Oh. I see." He looked away and flexed his knee, wincing. "Look, I liked your sister and I didn't know your dad, but she spoke of him as being her hero. If he came to our house intending to kill my brother, he deserves to be in prison, but I don't hold that against you or Diane."

Emery felt her eyes fill again. Her father was her hero

too. Still, in spite of everything. "Your brother and sister-in-law don't share your views."

"They don't share my views on a lot of things. At least we agree on the business stuff, mostly. I'll talk to Kevin. He's not going to bother you again if he wants to keep his job with us."

"Thank you," Emery said.

Roman nodded his thanks.

Mason tested his leg. "I'm going to pay for my clumsiness, I guess. Not sure I can drive myself to the ranch for our meeting." He rolled his eyes. "Embarrassing."

"I'll drive you." Emery blushed when Roman and Mason stared at her. "I mean, um, unless you'd rather not ride with me. Beth asked me to pick up some baby blankets so I might as well do that now before I go home and I can drop you off for the meeting."

Mason looked startled for a moment. "Okay. Thanks. I'll arrange for someone to pick up my car when it's convenient. Roman, I'll see you at the ranch. I wasn't planning on our meeting starting this way, but as long as it gets done, right?"

Roman still looked uncertain, probably wondering why she'd volunteered. She didn't know why she had either, except she had a burning desire to tell Mason what was in her heart.

"I'll follow as soon as I get the police on the phone," Roman said.

"Should I wait here too, to talk to them?" Emery said.

Roman shook his head. "No. Could take a while for them to arrive and there's not much to see, anyway. You go on to the ranch."

In case there was someone else around with another rock? She suppressed a shiver.

"I'll text the family to let them know you're on your way."

She quickly messaged Gino as well, relieved to hear that Ian was still asleep and Gino was enjoying a bowl of instant oatmeal he'd found in the pantry.

They buckled in. Mason chuckled. "At least I can tell my brother I got a sprint in today. He's always trying to curb my couch potato tendencies."

She laughed. "Lincoln's into fitness, I've noticed."

"Like you wouldn't believe. Me? I'd rather drive than run any day of the week." He surveyed the interior, neat but worn. He was no doubt accustomed to finer vehicles. They drove by his ride, a pristine Ford Fairlane.

He surveyed the interior of the borrowed car. "This color reminds me of the Thunderbird. That was my dad's pride and joy, and he taught me and Lincoln how to drive in it. Not worth much with all the dings and scuffs, but man, I have a soft spot for that old thing." He patted the dash. "This machine's got a great engine. Change the oil every three thousand miles and it will run forever."

His easy manner gave her courage. "Mr. Taylor…"

"Mason."

"Mason, while we have a minute, I want to say I am sincerely sorry for what happened. It seems so inadequate, in light of your injury. But if my father…"

Mason cocked his head. "If…? You think your father is innocent?"

She blushed. "I do. In your statement, you said you didn't actually see him pull the trigger. It was dark. There was a flash and you woke up to find EMS people there."

"That's true, but if your father didn't do it…" He blinked. "Oh. I see. So you believe your sister probably shot me, thinking I was Lincoln, and your father took the blame to protect her. His confession was bogus."

"I don't know. I really don't, but if she did, or if my father took the shot, I am so sorry for your pain and suffering."

"You've suffered too." He jerked a thumb at the chipped glass. "Seems like you still are and you didn't have a thing to do with my injury. Could be we both paid the price for our siblings, right? I'm going to guess you've been cleaning up after Diane's messes for a while, haven't you?"

She blushed. *It's when I stopped helping that things turned catastrophic.* "You could say that."

"And now you've got a baby. Believe it or not, I understand being the person that has to watch from afar while your sibling trashes their life. My brother had a great woman by his side. Hilary would have forgiven his overspending and mismanagement of the car collection, but she couldn't exactly turn a blind eye to his infidelity, now could she? They could have had an amazing life but he threw it away. What a waste."

"I can understand why Hilary is resentful."

"I am too, in some ways. Lincoln inherited the car collection from our father, and instead of growing the business, he sold off cars to pay his debts for school, et cetera. Hilary and I finally convinced him to build a showroom, but by then he was deep in debt and he had to sell more cars and finance the inn so there'd be a place for visitors to stay." He leaned against the headrest. "I love my brother and I'll support him to his grave, but the guy has no mind for business. It's hard not to resent it, right? Having to be your sibling's keeper?"

"Yes, it is." On that subject they could commiserate.

Suddenly he looked pained. "I shouldn't be talking badly

about my brother, especially to you. I hope you won't think my whole family is your enemy."

Only if they'd been responsible for driving her off the road and trying to drown her. Maybe Lincoln wasn't what he seemed, an arrogant womanizer. Diane had seen something in him, hadn't she? She remembered the feeling of plunging into the icy water with her wrists and feet bound. Mason was friendly, but blood was thicker than water and there was no reason to trust him completely. His priority was his family. She felt the same. She'd delivered her apology and that was the important thing.

She thanked him and they turned into the drive to the Security Hounds Ranch. This would be a quick drop off, snag the blankets from Beth and get back to her packing.

She parked.

Mason shot her a look, fingers on the door handle. "Hilary says she doesn't think Ian is Lincoln's, but deep down I wonder what she believes. What do you think?"

"I'm not sure. I know he's Diane's, and that's all that's important to me right now."

"Fair enough." Mason pushed the door open. "But if the baby is Lincoln's, he should help."

Emery puzzled as she got out. Did Hilary think Diane was telling the truth about Ian?

She remembered Hilary's forceful demeanor. She must have been humiliated by Lincoln's infidelity. What did she stand to lose if Lincoln really was Ian's father?

NINE

Roman had left a message with the police. Didn't matter. He'd be able to provide a face-to-face rundown with Hagerty who was also expected to attend the ranch meeting. He wouldn't put it past Kevin to have launched the rock at Emery. Rock throwing, the same kind of juvenile thing he himself might have done as an angry teen, exuding rage from every pore. *Until Theo straightened me out.* Was it progress that he could acknowledge the good Theo had done in his life?

He swallowed and confronted the thought instead of pushing it away.

Theo showed him another way and introduced him to the Wolfes. Emery's words echoed in his mind.

This might rock your world but I'd love him just as much if he was guilty.

And hadn't Roman himself been loved when he was angry and unlovable? By Theo? And the Wolfes? And his uncle? And God? He rubbed his eyes, gritty from lack of sleep.

And Emery thought he was helping her purely out of pity. Not true. Pity wasn't causing his stomach to knot when she was out of sight, or his blood to warm when she was near. It was something else that he didn't want to mull over at the moment. Why did Emery make him *think* so much?

As he parked next to her loaner car and the Taylors' gleaming Mercedes, his mental gears switched quickly. Lincoln, Mason and Hilary were talking to Officer Hagerty, Stephanie and Garrett. Beth had moved closer to Emery, protectively almost, probably realizing the awkwardness of the situation. Bad start. Somehow he was going to have to make this meeting work. If the Taylors or Hagerty weren't satisfied with the plan he'd laid out, they might drop the whole K-9 component from the car show altogether.

Not gonna let that happen.

Roman rubbed Wally in that special spot under his collar. He'd already slipped on the snazzy Security Hounds harness, which fit the bulky bloodhound perfectly. "Walls, I'm counting on you, baby. Don't let me down." He hoped Wally didn't know he was worried. This was, after all, the breakfast-snatching, pacifier-chewing dog with the brilliant nose and a dubious work ethic. That's why they'd be showcasing Chloe, their undisputed champion.

Wally whined, looking as if he wanted to go exploring. Roman took his collar and urged him into the fenced area with Chloe. Wally fired a "you are ruining my life" look at him.

Roman greeted everyone genially. Stephanie whispered in his ear, "'Bout time you got here. Mason's been telling us what happened at the garage. I want more details. And Hagerty has something for us, he said."

"I'll explain later. Everything set?"

Garrett's quick smile was affirmation.

Time to shine, bloodhounds.

Emery pursed her lips uneasily. "You've all got a busy

morning. How about I snag those blankets and get out of your hair?"

Hilary seemed as if she thought that was a grand idea. Lincoln was careful to avoid looking at Emery altogether. His body language telegraphed his desire to be anywhere but in her presence.

"Oh, no scooting out now. You'll want to see this," Beth said brightly. "Won't take long and the dogs have been working like…well, dogs."

Roman heard the velvety steel in his mom's voice. Emery had nothing to be ashamed of, she silently declared, daring with her bold eye contact for anyone to contradict her. No one did.

"Yes," he said, gaze riveted on Emery. She had every right to stay. Her father had helped the ranch stay afloat. Second time today he'd thought of Theo in a more positive way. Odd. "Stay. Please." Before she could reply, he dove into the itinerary.

"For the final event at the showroom on Sunday, we'll have a volunteer hidden in one of your cars," Roman said. "We'll do a quick talk for the guests while the dogs are well away from the showroom, then have them pick in which car she should conceal herself."

"Ah. To make sure there's no trickery," Hagerty said.

"Yes," he confirmed. "We'll give the dogs a scent article and have them track the guest." Two dogs, in case Wally decided he wasn't in the mood.

"All right, that's perfect for the day when the heavy buying will occur." Hilary surveyed the large fenced space where Chloe and Wally were nosing about. The other four were enjoying a nap in their kennels. They needed it, judging from the half dozen freshly dug holes he'd have to fill in after the demonstration. Canine backhoes, the lot of them.

He prayed Chloe and Wally would put on a stellar performance for the observers.

"But what about the day before?" Hilary demanded. "That's a nice demo for Sunday, but I'm billing this as a weekend stay for my inn so what's the Saturday entertainment?"

Lincoln finally looked up. "Saturday night we're auctioning off a Rolls so we want all the high rollers there." And Lincoln had pledged a portion of the proceeds to fund the new bloodhound county K-9 team, so Roman had planned an especially dramatic demo. His palms went clammy.

"Glad you asked," Roman said. "Saturday's demo will be something really unusual, including the inn, the estate and the ranch. Lincoln, you said you could show a live feed on the big screen in your showroom?"

He nodded. "Sure. I have top-of-the-line technology."

"Excellent. The Inn at the Pines is two miles from here. Hilary will have already chosen one of her guests to be a volunteer and someone from Security Hounds will accompany that individual to a hiding spot somewhere between our ranch and the inn. We'll put a GoCam on the bloodhound and while the rest of the attendees are enjoying the luncheon buffet you're providing at your estate, they can watch in real time as the dogs track down the guest."

Hagerty raised an eyebrow. "What if the dogs can't do it?"

"Not an issue. They can." Stephanie nodded emphatically.

"No question," Garrett added.

"And we'll have a table on your property so we can be handing out donation info for those who'd like to contribute toward funding our bloodhound team in the county." His mouth went so dry he almost couldn't get it out.

Emery caught his attention. He risked a quick glance at her and she gave him an almost imperceptible nod. Was she proud of him?

"All right," Hagerty said. "So that's two pretty ambitious events. Give us a preview. Let's see your star dogs in action to convince us this is going to work." He gave Roman a close look. "Time's marching on and I need to go take a look at the mechanic's shop, dispatch tells me."

Roman nodded. Later. No need to elaborate with Hilary and Lincoln within earshot. They'd hear it all from Mason, no doubt. "Garrett, can you take the dogs to the run for a minute?"

Garett whistled to the dogs who ambled amiably after him around the corner where they'd installed a covered area to be used during inclement weather. Bored and under-exercised bloodhounds were something to be avoided at all costs.

"He'll give them a treat and some water so they won't hear anything." Roman turned to Hilary. "Would you mind volunteering?"

"Me?"

"Our scents are all over this area so the dogs would have a hard time sorting out which trail to follow. They'll need to smell something you've touched. Your purse or scarf, your cell phone."

She took a silver container from her pocket. "How about this? My business card holder."

"Perfect." Roman pulled a bag from his pocket and asked her to drop it in. "We've got cars parked at the bottom of the road, one by the river on our property and a third beyond the kennels. Which one would you like to hide in?"

She cocked her head. "I've got to interview a new chef today. I don't have time for a long hike."

"The bottom of the road, then. That's a half mile and change, but it's downhill."

"I can do it. That's a short run for me." Lincoln said.

Hilary sniffed. "Oh, please. I'll walk. I don't run the mile in six minutes like you do, Lincoln, but I'm no slouch."

"True," Mason put in. "I've gone running with her and I practically need a taxi to keep up."

She quirked a smile at him. "You do fine as long as I give you a head start."

Mason grinned. "I'll hold down the fort from here. Record it on your cell phone so I can watch later, okay?"

Beth handed Mason and Lincoln binoculars. "These should help."

Stephanie messaged Garrett who returned with Chloe and Wally after Hilary was well away.

Roman clipped them both to long leads and gave them a whiff of Hilary's business card case still in the bag. Stephanie took Chloe's leash.

"Find." Chloe and Wally started in, sniffing in seemingly random circles. Roman let them both satisfy themselves before he gave them another smell. "Find," he repeated. Both dogs snuffled at the scent trail Hilary had left on the road.

Come on, dogs. You can do this. No sweat.

Emery gave him a thumbs-up and Garrett started a stopwatch.

The noisy snuffling, half-frantic parade began. Chloe's pursuit was methodical and straightforward, while Wally got sidetracked by a chittering squirrel and required firm redirecting. Stephanie and Chloe moved ahead.

Sixteen minutes later they arrived at the car, partially concealed by shrubbery. Hilary wasn't visible. Embracing her role, she'd crouched down below the windows. He smiled to himself. You could fool a bloodhound's eyes, but it was nearly impossible to trick their noses. The dogs both jumped up and barked eagerly, until he and Stephanie commanded them to sit. They did so reluctantly, taking the small treats but craving their real reward, the target they'd been tasked to pursue. Wally let loose with a victory howl the moment Hilary emerged from the car, slinging a trail of saliva as he did so.

"All right, I'm convinced," Hilary said. "You've got two fuzzy Sherlock Holmes detectives there, but they sure do drool a lot. It's gross."

He held back his own yowl of relief and pride and supplied more treats to the dogs before they all walked back to the house.

Beth and Emery clapped at their arrival and Garrett gave each dog a thorough scratch behind the neck.

"Record time," Beth said.

Mason nodded. "Even through the binocs, that was cool."

And Wally had actually completed the mission, squirrel notwithstanding, Roman thought with relief. Extra playtime and maybe some poached salmon was in order.

"Impressive," Lincoln said. "The guests will eat it up with a spoon."

And hopefully donate to the cause. Chloe sprawled happily at Stephanie's feet but Wally avoided Roman's attempts to put him into a sit. Still amped up on the adrenaline possibly? He whined and pulled at the leash.

Hilary collected her business card case. "Let's go, Lincoln. I've got things to do. I'll drop you in town and you can drive Mason back."

Roman moved to let them by and Wally seized the moment to follow his nose around the parked cars.

"Walls, come on," Roman said, hoping the dog would listen.

He didn't. When Wally was fixed on a scent, Roman could have been hollering into a megaphone and the dog would still ignore him. He'd galumphed right up to the driver's side door of the Mercedes. Wally's wide behind was blocking Lincoln's access.

Lincoln's lip curled. "Can you move your dog, please?"

"Wally," he said sternly, feeling the mortification rising. The dog glided his nose over the shiny metal.

"He's not going to scratch the paint, is he?" Hilary said.

Not now. Don't show them your disobedient side. There's no way they'll let you in that showroom with all those expensive cars. But Wally would not be dissuaded. His nose left a wet spot on the shiny paint. Roman was about to grab the dog and hoist him aside when Emery stepped close.

"Wally," Emery said. She had her back to the people but Roman saw Wally's attention snap from the Mercedes toward Emery. "Come with me, little man." As if in a trance, he trotted after her and onto the porch.

Roman tried to hide his shock. Wally was taking orders from Emery as if they'd worked together for years. He closed his mouth and waved goodbye to the departing visitors.

Officer Hagerty lingered. "Got something for you."

"Come inside," Beth said. "I'll make coffee."

"I will never say no to a good cup of coffee. Station stuff tastes like we brewed it in a carburetor."

Roman hustled up to Emery where she still crouched next to Wally.

"I have to know. How did you get him to cooperate?"

She opened her hand, revealing a blue plastic pacifier, which Wally immediately began to lick, his tail whipping in happy arcs. "I bought an extra when we stopped at the store. Figured you needed it for Wally more than I needed a spare for Ian."

He laughed. She joined in. For a moment a mountain was removed from his shoulders and he guffawed with everything in him until they both ran out of air. "I owe you, big-time."

"Yep, you still owe me an ice cream and now another favor. Really racking up the debt, Wolfe."

There was nothing more lovely than her pluck, her humor, her light. No rock-thrower, abductor or hateful townsperson had dulled the spark she carried. He held out his hand and she took it. He pulled her to her feet and she delivered the pacifier. They let Wally enjoy it for a few minutes before Roman retrieved it.

"If you're a good boy, maybe Roman will let you have some quality time with your paci later, okay?" Emery crooned.

Seemingly content, Wally let Roman usher him into the gated yard where he joined Garret's dog Pinkerton in excavating a new trench.

"While you're here, see if Hagerty needs any more details about what happened at the garage."

The remark made her go quiet. He felt pinpricks of rage that someone had attempted to injure her again. What if Ian had been in the car? Thinking of harm coming to either one of them was intolerable. His pace quickened as they marched for the house until she put a hand on his arm.

"Slow down," she said. "I'm getting a cramp."

"Sorry." He tucked her arm through his and it felt like the most natural thing in the world. He decided to enjoy it and let his brain relax for a moment. It might have been his imagination, but he thought she relaxed too, her shoulder pressed to his.

Hagerty was halfway through the coffee Beth had presented him when they entered. Kara was there too, wan and thinner than she seemed only a week before. He noted his mother's worried glance and knew she'd noticed too.

"Hey, K.K.," he said as she curled up cross-legged on the sofa with her laptop over her knees. Barefoot, practically always when inside, even in winter. "How are things going with the case you and Chase are working?"

She accepted his kiss on the cheek. "Chase is wrapping up but I think we have enough to send to the client. His tenant is definitely using the property to move stolen goods."

"Did Tank perform okay?"

"Like a champion, which Chase will tell you all about when he gets back." She looked at Emery. "I'm sorry about what happened in town." She reached out a hand and gripped Emery's. Some understanding seemed to pass between them. Kara knew what it was like to be on the outside looking in.

"Sit here." She patted the sofa next to her and Emery settled in.

"So about the rock-throwing business…" Hagerty said. "We got a confession from Kevin."

Emery sighed. "He was sending me a 'get out of town' message."

Hagerty slugged down some coffee. "Might not be a bad idea. We found a GPS tracker on the rear wheel well of your car. That's how someone knew you were in Whisper Valley."

Her face paled. "Someone's been tracking me?"

Hagerty nodded. "They probably put it on at your apartment would be my guess."

Roman felt a cold chill. Emery had been hunted even before she arrived in town.

Her lip quivered for a moment. "I can't. I have to pack up my father's house. It's being foreclosed. My sister and dad are both in the hospital so there's no one left to do it, otherwise I'd take your advice in a heartbeat, believe me."

Her comment pained Roman. Totally reasonable that she'd want to leave at the first possible opportunity, wasn't it?

Hagerty drank more coffee. "A bad look for Whisper Valley. I'll see what I can find out, but I'm pretty certain it won't be much." He looked at Kara. "Did you get it?"

She nodded and tapped her screen.

Hagerty explained. "Emailed the video of the car that went after us, at least the two seconds my body cam caught before we hit the dirt."

Kara pulled it up on her screen.

"Can you—?" Roman started but she'd already patched it through to the TV. They stood closer to get a better look as Kara froze the frame. He found his shoulder brushing Emery's again and he resisted the urge to loop his arm around her. That didn't stop him from enjoying the light floral scent of her freshly washed hair. He remembered the hot summer between her junior and senior year of high school when she'd let her long waves dry in the sun while she visited the ranch. He'd found it fascinating, the heavy weight of her thick mane and how it would curl as it dried. Same slight curl in it now. Maybe since her cover had been blown, she'd let it return to its natural blond hue. He hoped so. No store-bought color could ever compare.

Would you focus already?

"No license plate or even a partial," Hagerty said. "As you can see, all we got is the front right of a black vehicle, tire impressions indicate it's a quality ride."

"Did your people conclude anything else?" Garrett asked.

"Nope. All over to you hotshot detectives now."

Roman didn't take offense at the tease. Hagerty had made good on his promise to share information with Security Hounds and that was a victory. "The front end plowed through the ground pretty hard. Likely got some scratches or dings."

Hagerty nodded. "Thought of that, but I don't have time to chase it down."

"We do," Beth said.

"For sure." Stephanie turned to her sister. "Kara, if you can get me some names of car detailers or body shops in the area, I'll do the legwork."

Garrett raised his hand. "I'll help."

They settled into a moment of uneasy silence. Roman knew his siblings understood where his mind had drifted.

"Spill it," Hagerty said. "Tell me what you're thinking."

"Wally was real interested in Lincoln's Mercedes."

He looked at Roman over the edge of his mug. "Thought he was just being a pain."

"He was, but he also might be recalling the scent from the car that almost ran us down."

All eyes riveted on Roman.

"You're not saying Lincoln Taylor tried to kill us?" Hagerty said.

"Just noting that Wally's reaction is curious. The car's pristine, like it'd been recently washed and detailed, right down to the tires."

"The Taylors are car people. It's their livelihood. They're not gonna ride around in dirty vehicles. They probably have a detailing facility on the property. And I know for a fact they own several Mercedes."

Roman didn't reply to Hagerty's comment.

Beth said, "Lincoln Taylor, Hilary, Kevin the mechanic, other staff people at the estate, I'm sure they all had access to the car. It could have been cleaned on site or taken elsewhere."

"Uh-huh." Hagerty put down his empty mug. "Not the greatest business move to imply someone connected to the Taylors is a criminal."

Roman hoped his tone was neutral. "Not implying. Sharing Wally's reaction is all."

Hagerty peered out the living room window. Wally was almost up to his tail in the crater he'd dug. He was churning up a blizzard of soil with his sturdy paws. "Trust that hound, do you?"

Stephanie's expression was highly amused as she watched for Roman's response. Did he trust Wally? Hadn't he been trying to offload the stubborn animal before he'd rescued Emery from drowning? He kept his sister confined to his peripheral vision and opened his mouth to answer.

"For what it's worth, I do." Emery's comment startled him. She offered Hagerty a bright smile. "He saved us in the lake, found my car and alerted us in time to keep all three of us from being mowed down. I trust him."

Roman stood a little straighter and fought hard to keep the grin from his face. He tried to put the feelings aside and focus on the case but as he caught sight of his filthy dog sprawled on a patch of sunlit grass, he felt a great surge of affection. Wally might be stubborn and prone to following his own drum, but Roman had the deep-down conviction that the hound had detected something invisible to the rest of them on Lincoln's car.

Was it the same vehicle that had almost run them down? Hopefully Kara's investigations would help discover the truth. In the meantime he intended to keep a very close eye on Emery and Ian.

Hagerty finally nodded. "When you put it that way, I guess I owe him too. I'll keep in mind what you've said and we'll put our info together after you do some of the legwork. I'm sure you'll be discreet, since you're not law enforcement and all..."

A shadow crossed Garrett's face but he beamed a smile anyway. "We are the soul of discretion. Ask anyone. We fly totally under the radar."

"Right. You and your noisy pack of slobbering hounds." Hagerty checked the time on his watch. "I'll talk to you all later."

Beth walked him to the door. "Thank you for coming, Officer. Our coffeepot is at your disposal any time." When he left, she clasped a hand to her lower back. Roman hastened to grab an ice pack from the freezer, knowing she would put it off until they'd left the room.

She shot him a tired half smile. "Thank you, Roman."

She sank onto the sofa and his worries came back in a rush. They had to make the K-9 event work. Had he jeopardized everything with his suspicions before they'd gotten anything resembling proof?

Kara's gaze shifted to Roman and her siblings. "So... I'm looking into this? We're investigating the Taylors?"

Roman blew out a breath. "I don't want to jeopardize our arrangement with them but..."

"I don't want a partnership with anyone who's ready to hurt to get what they want," Beth snapped. "If they're guilty, we need to know." She cocked her chin at Emery. "We'll try to keep you out of this as much as possible, but Security Hounds is diving into this case because we need answers." She was every inch the in-charge flight nurse

in that moment before her tone softened. "Do you understand, Emery?"

Emery's shoulders sagged. Was she finally resigned to
having Security Hounds officially involved? "I want answers too," she said. "I know you aren't looking specifi-
cally for proof that my father isn't guilty, but I can't help
feeling this all circles back to that night."

That night...when everything had changed for him, her,
Theo, Diane, Ian and Mason.

What really happened in those dangerous moments?
With Security Hounds involved, maybe they'd be able to
put it all to rest.

"We'll need to go over the details again," Garrett said.
"Everything you can recall. I'll contact Hagerty for the
police reports, Mason's statement, your father's confession, et cetera."

"This is painful," Beth said. "I'm sorry, and honestly
I pray that we'll be able to turn up something that might
help you and Theo."

Emery's lower lip quivered.

Would they uncover proof of Theo's guilt so even Emery
would believe it? Or maybe Diane was the guilty party?
Roman's stomach squirmed. Wasn't it possible that things
weren't what they seemed where her father was concerned?

She'd love him anyway. That thought spun slowly
through his mind like a bird floating on the wind. She
spoke of an unconditional love, a love closer to the perfect
love that God offered. Loving through disappointment.

He thought of Uncle Jax.

"Roman?"

His mother's question zapped him back. He realized
everyone's attention had slid to him, waiting to see his reaction. They knew how crushed he'd been at Theo's confes-

sion. Did he want to open that poorly healed scab? Confront the feelings he kept buried beneath his reticence?

No, he didn't. He wanted nothing to do with any of it. There were plenty of problems on today's plate without revisiting agonizing history. But the need to defend his Wolfe family, if necessary, and Emery, was more important than his wish to dodge his own pain.

Emery was the true victim in all this, and the baby she was struggling to care for.

His discomfort was trivial. A predator was stalking her. If he had to, he'd fight through the pain and protect them both, no matter what the cost.

He gave one slow nod.

Security Hounds was 100 percent in…and so was he.

TEN

At Beth's direction, Kara fetched the blankets. Emery tucked the soft fleece under her arm, thanked them and promised to make herself available as best she could in between packing and baby care. Reality weighed her down. As much as she wanted to assist with anything that might shed light on her father's confession, she had an entire cabin to pack up in a week's time. Beth waved a goodbye from the sofa.

The pain must be intense to keep the strong woman down.

Roman seemed lost in thought as he walked her to the car until she squeezed his arm.

"Sorry, I was thinking." He snagged a look at her. "Why are you smiling?"

"It's an appreciative smile."

"Appreciative of what?"

She shrugged, cheeks warm. "The way you suggested investigating the Taylors' car."

He looked at the sky and then back at her. The light bronzed his neatly cut hair. She'd always thought the ginger color was glorious, though she'd lacked the courage to tell him so. Probably never would.

"Emery, I don't want you to jump to conclusions. The most likely scenario is still…"

She waved away the rest of his comment. "I know… that my dad is guilty of attempted murder and the threats on my life are unrelated, but you were willing to speak up to Hagerty."

He shrugged. "Being thorough is all. Your safety's in question."

"Not just thorough, you're taking a risk since you're business partners with the Taylors at the moment. I know you have a lot riding on the deal."

His mouth tightened and he stroked a hand over his chin. "Mom needs back surgery. As I mentioned, because of the expense and recovery time, she won't agree until the business is more secure. Tough lady."

"That's why she was a good flight nurse."

"Stubborn."

"The perfect pack leader for a bunch of tenacious Wolfes. It's terrible to see her in such pain."

A flicker of worry crossed his face. "I can't stand it either. She's finally let me take over some of her chores, hauling the food bags and such, but there's no way past the pain unless she has the surgery." He paused. "I more or less put all our eggs into this basket, hoping to get a contract deal with the county for bloodhound services. My sibs don't all agree that it was the right choice. This car show's our best shot, probably our only one."

"And you were willing to jeopardize that? For me?"

"For the truth."

Of course, that was the reason. Why had she even said that?

He straightened to his full six feet and change, shoulders broad and muscled. "Did you think I'd ignore some-

thing criminal to protect the interests of the ranch? Is that
the kind of man you think I am?"

She went still, stung by his irritation. He was offended
that she'd besmirched his honor? "No, but I don't exactly
know you well anymore, do I?" The slight reproach in her
tone was no doubt clear to him. She could tell in the tight-
ening of his jaw. *Remember who you're dealing with.* Before she'd almost been drowned, she'd seen him only long
enough for him to walk away.

Is it true that your father shot a man in cold blood?

Once Roman had been the hero in her heart, the hand-
some young man who could do everything from building
kennels to mountain climbing, and always with a joke or
a tease. But now they were grown-ups and she'd taken off
her rose-colored glasses. He'd stepped out of her life, along
with everyone else, and it hurt. She hadn't realized how
deeply until she'd returned to Whisper Valley.

Affection and admiration warred with the bitter echoes
of disappointment. He despised her father, maybe just as
much as the rock-thrower, the notion of forgiveness as
distant and inaccessible as the Cascades. The realization
landed on her like a falling tree. Her father's guilt or inno-
cence wasn't the reason for the hurt that spiraled through
her. "You know Roman, no matter what you thought about
Dad, I could have used your friendship."

He recoiled as if she'd slapped him. "You didn't want
me there…" His words died away. His shoulders fell as he
heaved out a breath. "I should have stuck around for you,
no matter how I felt. I was so wrapped up in my own hurt
I didn't consider yours. I'm sorry, Emery."

Her eyes flew wide. He'd apologized? She was struggling to come up with a reply when they reached the car
and he yanked open the driver's door for her. "As far as

the Taylors go, if someone in that household had a role in dumping you in the lake, they're going to pay the price."

And that was something else to marvel at. Roman had not only apologized for the past, but he was willing to wade into her situation, no matter how much it upset him. She felt a surge of gratitude poke through the uncertainty. "I hope it doesn't cost you much, helping me."

He looked at her full-on then, reached out and brushed the hair from her cheek. "You've paid a higher price than anyone, Ree."

The nickname, the touch, the look, no anger there, only sorrow and determination. Her heart warmed as she slid behind the wheel of the borrowed car. She felt her phone buzz. Panic nearly overtook her as she recognized the number and answered.

Gino's breathless voice ratcheted her nerves. "Ian's fine, but we have a problem."

Another one? She put it on speaker. "Roman's with me on this call. What's wrong?"

She could hear the drapes rustle as Gino answered.

"There are reporters here. Two of them."

Her stomach knotted up. "Oh, no. This is not what we need right now."

"I didn't speak to them, except to tell them to go away, but they shouted a few questions at me. They're still there, camped next to the driveway."

Emery's spirits dropped with every word. "What did they ask you?"

"Can't you guess? They found out you're in town and smelled a spicy story. They didn't mention your escape from the lake, but they probably caught wind of it. Possibly they're apprised about the foreclosure too. Public record. They asked about the baby."

How was she going to keep Ian out of the limelight now? He'd be a target of hatred too. She leaned her forehead against the steering wheel. "This is all spinning out of control."

Roman took the phone from her hand. "Any way you can get out with Ian and come here?"

"Not without being swarmed," Gino said. "Ian's real fussy at the moment so it's hard for me to think. He won't take his bottle."

Emery sat up. "I'm leaving right now. I'll be there in a half hour."

"But how will you get by—?" Gino asked.

She cut him off, her tone savage. "It's still my father's house, at least for another week, anyway. I'll call the police if they block my way. Sit tight and try the bouncy seat with Ian, okay? Sometimes that helps."

She disconnected, tried to gather her thoughts. The last thing she wanted was to face down hungry journalists. She'd done enough of that when her father had first been arrested. In her present state of mind, she couldn't predict what would come out of her mouth if she were confronted. Roman stood watching her, thumbs tucked into his belt.

"I'd better go," she said.

He reached through the window and touched her forearm. "Give me one second to grab Wally. I've got a plan."

"What kind of plan?"

He smiled, a boyish grin. "Wally and I are going to be decoys."

Decoys? "How exactly is that going to work?"

"We'll drive right on up to the front, bold as brass. The reporters don't know you're in a borrowed car. You can take the fire trail from the south and park in the woods behind the cabin. I've used that path to train Wally before.

The trail leads all the way up to Tule Lake but you can pull off about a quarter mile past the cabin and loop around. It's a short drive to the house. I checked it all out when we first got there."

She gaped at his cunning. "What will you say to the reporters?"

He grinned, a flash of the mischievous teen. "I'll let Wally do the talking."

As much as she wanted to stand up for herself, to send all those reporters packing through her sheer force of will, Roman's offer sent sweet relief coursing through her. She was tired, frightened and feeling more and more desperate to get back to Ian.

"See you in a few. I'll stay for a while and help pack."

"But you've got to—"

He leaned close and kissed her. His lips were soft and warm against hers.

"Help you," he finished. "That's all I'm going to worry about right now. Wait here."

Stunned, she watched him jog away. Her mouth tingled from the kiss.

He was sorry for their past. Willing to put himself out for her safety and Ian's. Perhaps risk the future of the ranch.

What was going on?

And why was her heart skipping as she watched him go?

With Emery departing fifteen minutes ahead of them, Roman opened the window halfway so Wally could shove his head out. The wind sent his ears flapping like giant propellers. The dog went so far as to open his jaws and let the breeze inflate his cavernous mouth, gulping in the air as if it were a juicy steak.

"You're turning into a halfway decent dog, Walls. That was some performance, finding Hilary."

The dog turned from his entertainment long enough to twitch a saggy brow at him as if to say, "I know." He considered Wally's reaction to the Taylors' Mercedes. Might be nothing at all. That happened sometimes with bloodhounds. They were attracted to every imaginable scent unless they were encouraged to focus on a particular search. Might be a stray odor from a take-out bag or another dog that had been transported in the car. Then again, what if one of the Taylors had been behind the wheel and tried to plow them down?

But what could possibly be the motive?

Something to do with the shooting six months earlier? It couldn't be, yet his gut would not dismiss the thought. He'd trained plenty of army soldiers and their dogs, and if there was an underlying theme, it had to be *trust your dog and your squad.*

He trusted his Wolfe squad, and he was slowly coming to trust Wally. The Taylors were business partners only.

What about Emery?

He wasn't sure what had prompted him to apologize to her, though it had been exactly right. A God thing, probably. That straightened him up. Interesting, since he hadn't felt very connected to God for a long time. He squeezed and relaxed his fingers on the steering wheel. Maybe Emery's assertion that she'd love her father even if he was guilty had started things percolating inside his own soul. For years he'd thought he'd had a right to his grudge against Uncle Jax, but the adult Roman understood that he'd been the one to walk away from his uncle, not the other way around. And he'd walked away from Emery too.

Man, the growing up thing was torture sometimes.

He forced his mind to the details of the Security Hounds demonstration. All the dogs would need baths. That'd be a messy undertaking. The doggy aroma was already thick in the vehicle in spite of the open window.

"If you'd keep away from Mom's chicken coop, you'd smell better, you know."

Wally whacked him with his thick tail as the drive to Theo's cabin came into view. Parked on the rocky shoulder were two vehicles with men in the driver's seats. When they heard Roman's approach, they both got out, phones ready to record. He slowed to give them time to get closer.

Wally eyed them with curiosity.

"You ready for your big moment, boy?" He flicked the radio to the country station. The change in Wally was instantaneous. He yanked his head inside the vehicle and sat in a tidy bundle, nose pointed to the radio. Three, two, one...

As soon as Roman edged up the volume, Wally broke into a plaintive yowl.

The reporters hesitated.

Wally did not. His soulful accompaniment to the music grew so loud Roman's ears pulsed. He rolled down his window as the men drew abreast. "Afternoon."

They introduced themselves, but he only caught a few words. He tapped his ear. "Sorry, can't hear you. Dog's a real performer."

"Can you tell us if Emery Duncan is here?" the taller one shouted. "Does she have her sister's baby with her?"

"What?" Roman said.

Wally started in on the next song with gusto. The howling actually vibrated the glass. Impressive.

The shorter one said something that sounded like a rude suggestion on how to shut Wally up. Roman kept his smile in place. "Hey, fellas. Sorry, but I can't control him when he wants to sing. A regular Pavarotti, you know? I'm just here to do some manual labor so I'd better get on that."

"But…" they both said at once.

Wally let loose with another ripping chorus. Roman pointed to his ear again and shrugged. "Catch you later, huh?"

He was still laughing when Gino let them into the cabin. He immediately shut and bolted the door.

Emery cradled the fussing baby, beaming a smile at him. "It worked, just like you said. They didn't see me come in the back."

He felt a rush of pleasure at her smile. Ian let loose with a scream and launched his pacifier into the air. Roman caught it, just before Wally did.

She laughed. "Thanks. Another excellent save."

Roman chuckled and handed it back to her. Their fingers brushed, hers warm, delicate. He wanted to clasp her palm in his. His heart thudded hard in his chest. "How about I, uh, pack? Should I start in the basement?"

She nodded.

Relieved to have a quiet place to marshal his unruly feelings, he grabbed some boxes and got to work.

When Emery was almost at her limit, Ian finally dropped into a late afternoon nap in his bouncy seat, which did not bode well for a restful night. Wally snoozed next to him, a comical sight. Emery's nerves were frazzled from comforting her fussy nephew and spending every free moment cramming her father's belongings into the cartons, while Gino did the same in the garage and Roman tackled the basement.

It hurt, boxing her father's possessions, the reels and the

piles of books about fly-fishing. Would he survive the heart attack? Spend the rest of his life in jail and never enjoy fishing again? Among a stack of unused envelopes, she found an unframed snapshot of her and Diane, knobby kneed in denim shorts, ankle deep in the mud, her dad photobombing behind them. It was the last family vacation she could remember. Tears fogged her vision as she knelt there. They were so happy in the picture, unaware of the traumas that would follow: divorce, her mother's departure, and now the unfathomable mess with her father, Diane's injury. Her fingers traced their young faces, her father's unruly hair. How had it all unraveled?

"No matter what, I still love you both," she said and though she felt sad, the anger was missing. She'd let go of the resentment against Diane, she realized. Sisters, for better or for worse. She wished she could tell Diane as much.

Warm breath on her neck made her jump. Wally pressed the advantage and licked her chin. She realized Roman was standing in the living room, a mug dangling from his index finger.

"Uh…sorry," he said. "I was craving some coffee, if you have any."

She jumped up. The pendulum clock on the wall read five thirty. "Oh, I'm sorry. I lost track of time. You're probably hungry. I'll fix some dinner."

"No need. I'm okay with coffee."

"You've been packing all day and we might as well eat while Ian's quiet. Trust me, it won't last long."

Roman set the table for three while she scrambled the eggs she'd got at the store and toasted slices of sourdough. Wally opened a baggy eye, nose twitching at the smell of food, but stayed snuggled up next to Ian.

"You didn't let him near Ian's pacifiers, did you? He'll have stolen them all if he got the chance."

She laughed and it felt good to be sharing an easy moment. "Ian prefers his thumb to his pacifier right now, so we're okay for the time being."

The phone rang while she was sliding the food onto plates and handing them to Gino.

"It's Kara." Roman put it on speaker. "You've got me, Emery and Gino. What did you find out?"

Kara's voice was soft so they all leaned forward to hear.

"No surprise that the local auto body shop indicated no repairs to a black Mercedes."

Roman nodded. "Taylors wouldn't risk getting the damage fixed in town."

"Right. There are three other shops within a fifty-mile radius. None was particularly interested in talking to me, but Stephanie took over. Either they didn't do the work, or they're covering up."

"So no progress," Roman sighed.

"There's another avenue," Kara said. "I'll let Stephanie tell you about it."

Stephanie launched in. "I did some digging at the jail."

Emery's eyes flew wide. "The jail?"

Gino repositioned the plates, brows knitted.

"I have a contact there. Unofficial, of course, but I was curious about Theo's activities."

Her father's activities in jail? She'd not anticipated that avenue of inquiry. She wanted to ask more questions, but she forced herself into the chair, mouth closed. She'd agreed to let the Wolfes investigate in whatever direction that took them, so she couldn't exactly complain about their decisions.

Gino voiced her thoughts a moment later. "What does this have to do with the danger to Emery?"

Stephanie seemed unaffected by Gino's clipped tone. "I don't know yet. Maybe nothing, but Theo apparently made calls on a regular basis to someone. My contact didn't know who and couldn't tell us anyway even if they did."

Emery's heart squeezed. Regular calls, yet her father steadfastly refused to speak to her, his daughter. Roman must have noticed her surge of grief because he sidled around and put a reassuring hand on her back.

"I wish I didn't have to revisit all this right now," she whispered, so low only Roman heard.

He bent and murmured in her ear. "Sorry, Ree. It'll be over soon."

His warmth prickled her skin in goose bumps.

Stephanie continued. "He scribbled lots of notes and my contact found one on the floor after one of his phone calls. Most of it was illegible except for *password.*"

"Password?" Emery balled up a napkin. "What could he be thinking?"

"No idea. Prisoners aren't allowed on the internet, so I'm not sure why he'd be focused on that word. I was going to ask if your dad was a big computer guy before…well, before," Stephanie said.

She rolled the napkin between her palms. "He wasn't. The opposite, really. It was always hard to get him to use the computer. But there's one in the basement, an iPad. Do you want me to…?" She caught a strange look from Roman. "What?"

"There isn't an iPad in the basement."

Her mouth fell open. "But…there was when I was down there before. You must have missed it."

Roman shook his head. "Feel free to double check me,

but I've packed almost everything down there and there's no iPad."

"Did you borrow it, Gino?"

He shook his head. "Nah."

Emery stood. "I'm going to look again. Can you watch Ian for a second, Gino?"

"Call you back in a minute," Roman told his sister.

Emery flipped on the light and they hurried down the steep staircase.

The air grew cooler with each step.

"It was on the..." She blinked in disbelief. The desk was now cleared off, the drawers partially open and empty. "You didn't see an iPad? Right there?" She traced her fingers over the scarred wood.

He shook his head slowly. "There were no computers down here."

A thought occurred to her and she pulled the desk away from the wall. He hurried to help.

"There," she said in triumph. A charging cord was plugged into the wall.

"Good detective work. So he had a device down here and a way to charge it." His eyes shaded from brown to black in the dim light as they found hers. "Who took it, then?"

"It wasn't Gino, if that's what you're thinking. He wouldn't lie."

Roman hesitated a beat. "Someone else got into the cabin since you arrived here?"

She went cold all over. A stranger might have been poking around. She thought of the shadowy figure she'd seen move past the basement window.

"I'm scared, Roman." The admission came out before she could stop it and she shivered.

He enveloped her in an embrace, tucking her under his

chin. "Let me stay the night here with you. Wally and I can sack out on the sofa."

"I can't ask."

"You didn't."

She pulled away to look at him. "And what if I say no?"

He sighed mournfully and pressed a hand to his heart in dramatic fashion. "Then poor Wally and I are in for an uncomfortable night, patrolling in the freezing cold every hour, trying to catch some shut-eye in my cramped Bronco, fending off attacks from packs of coyotes..."

She folded her arms, fighting down a smile. "The coyote thing was a tad over the top."

He raised a brow. "Should have gone with a pride of mountain lions?"

His mischievous look was so reminiscent of her teen heartthrob. On tiptoe she kissed him, a soft quick touch that thrilled through her and awakened a wondering look on his face. Why had she done that? Hastily she turned to the stairs to hide the blush. "Thank you, Roman."

"My pleasure," he said quietly.

ELEVEN

Roman felt a ridiculous swell of pride as he handed the baby over to Emery. "Took me sixteen laps but I finally got him to sleep."

Emery flashed him a weary smile. "My deepest gratitude. Let's hope he stays that way." She tiptoed away and laid him down in the porta crib before rejoining Roman and Wally.

"Where's Gino?"

"He's already gone to sleep, I think. Or he's out for a walk now that the reporters have decamped."

Roman refrained from commenting. Gino's behavior was suspect as far as he was concerned. It seemed more likely to Roman that Gino had taken the iPad than it was the work of a stranger. He couldn't fathom a motive.

She yawned, heading for the coffeepot. "I'll refuel and tackle the bookshelves."

"It can wait until morning."

"I wish. I only have a few days left to get this house packed up." He was going to argue but she waggled a finger at him. "And your event kicks off tomorrow so you need some sleep too."

The argument died on his lips. She was right. Tomorrow was a make-or-break day for Security Hounds, the moment when they'd hopefully prove their worth to the community and police department.

"Any way I can convince you to come stay at the ranch while the demonstration is in progress?" For safety reasons, he told himself, but there was some sensation that ballooned in his chest when she was near, a feeling he couldn't put words to, though he was beginning to crave it.

She smoothed her hair and his fingers longed to do the same.

"I have to get things straight here. It's the only thing I can do for Dad."

Her dad, his mentor, the prisoner. In the past the mere thought of Theo would have shot bitter anger through every nerve. Now he felt more subtle sorrow mixed with concern.

"What?" she said softly. "There's a funny look on your face."

"I, uh, was just thinking about your dad." He slouched, then straightened, unsure what to do with his hands. "How you said you'd love him anyway, guilty or innocent."

She nodded.

He lifted a shoulder. "He's blessed, is all, to have that kind of love." The room felt too small, his emotions far too big. "Gonna take Wally out." She didn't reply but he felt her gaze as he left.

Wally hustled outside, eagerly inhaling scents hidden from his handler. He cocked his head, ears trailing, nostrils quivering.

Roman tried to see what Wally was noting.

The quiet rustling of branches drew him. Wally beelined over and Roman caught up and put a hand on his collar. "Wait," he cautioned the dog, but he could feel the stocky body straining against his hold.

He eased forward to the other side of the shrubs but

found no one there. Had there been someone a moment before? Or some nocturnal creature who'd made the smart choice to flee from the exuberant bloodhound? Uneasy, he continued to prowl with no further signs that any intruders were in the vicinity.

His phone buzzed and he answered.

"You're up late," he said to Stephanie.

"Can't sleep. I could hear Mom trying to get comfortable in her recliner."

"She needs that surgery."

"Yes, more reason why the event has to be a smash. We've spent enough on it."

He felt the jab and the truth in it. "It'll pay off."

"Sure you'll be here ready to roll tomorrow?"

"Is that a serious question?" Truth be told, he might be awake all night, counting the minutes until morning.

"I've been researching the Taylor family. Patriarch Benjamin Taylor lost his wife to cancer when she was thirty-three. Put his life and blood into the cars he'd collected with the money he inherited from his father. Had a couple of major credit card debts when he died, which his sons had to pay off. Not the best business man is my impression."

"How's the outfit doing now?"

"Hard to say. They've added to their collection steadily, built a premier showroom and all that."

Roman considered. "Expensive."

"Very."

"What are you thinking, Steph?"

"That it'd be pricey to raise a kiddo too."

"Meaning?"

"Meaning that Diane was pressing Lincoln for a paternity test. Hilary had good reason for hating Diane on that count alone. If they wound up marrying, she wouldn't take that well. Mason might have wanted Diane out of the picture too if Lincoln is bleeding money and possibly adding a kid to the list of expenses."

"Yet we've still got Theo Duncan confessing to the crime and all the evidence pointing to him."

"Evidence can be manipulated."

He felt a thrill of hope. "You think Theo isn't guilty?"

"I don't know. That little tickle in the bottom of my stomach is telling me something is not what it appears to be."

"Keep digging."

"I will. See you tomorrow."

As he laid down on the sofa, he tried to stick to the practical, but for the first time since he'd heard of Theo's arrest, he realized how desperately he wanted Stephanie's suggestion to be true. What if all was not what it seemed?

But why would Theo refuse to say what he knew in favor of investigating from prison? Surely the police were more equipped to handle an investigation than an incarcerated guy. And why had he shut Emery out when she might have helped him? Troubling thoughts. He returned to the cabin.

Emery had fallen asleep in the armchair, the door to her bedroom open in case Ian cried out. Her expression was gentle, the worry lines faded away into peaceful rest. His heart lurched and he took the blanket and covered her.

She needed sleep and he and Wally did too if they were going to perform their best the next day, but it wouldn't hurt to pack up a few more boxes in the basement. If it would help her and Ian, he'd sacrifice. Plus he'd be awake and alert to any danger.

The notion comforted him and he found he was smiling as he headed down the staircase.

* * *

Wally's muffled baying startled Emery awake. Wally? What was he upset about? The clock read a few minutes after three in the morning. She didn't remember returning to the bedroom. Fear nibbled at the edges of her consciousness, shrilling an indistinct message until her senses kicked in. The acrid smell... Fire!

She leaped from the bed, landing hard on her knees before plunging toward the porta crib. Ian was still sleeping. Smoke wafted under the bedroom door.

"Gino, Roman," she screamed as she grabbed the baby. No answer.

"Roman," she screamed again.

She heard only her own frantic breathing. Covering the baby with a blanket, she put a finger on the doorknob. Cool to the touch, but when she tried to open it, the door wouldn't budge.

Dropping to her knees, she felt a piece of wood wedged in the jamb. She pounded with both fists. "Help."

She forced herself to think. The box cutter she'd been using to dispose of miscellaneous cardboard. It was on the chair. She snatched it up and quickly removed the pins from the door hinges, dropping them both and tugging with all her might on the knob. At first there was no movement, but the disabled hinge finally allowed her to yank the door inward.

The smoke was billowing from the rear of the house in ghostly puffs. Gino's door was open, his room empty. She checked the bathroom and found it empty too. Roman and Wally were not on the sofa. What had happened? Where were they?

Her next scream ratcheted up in volume.

This time there was a thump and a muffled shout before the basement door slammed open with a splintering of wood. Wally and Roman burst through. "Locked in. Wally smelled the smoke before I did. Where's Gino?"

"I don't know. He's not in his room, or the bathroom."

He pulled her to his side and reached for the baby. "Let me take him. Stay low. Crawl to the door." He tucked Ian inside his sweat jacket and zipped it closed.

The smoke made her cough, tears streaming until she couldn't see the way. She heard the kitchen curtains catch with a whoosh as the fire consumed the fabric. The doorframe was next for the gobbling flames. There would be no escape through the kitchen door.

"Hold on." He took her hand and wrapped it around Wally's harness.

"Away," he yelled to the dog.

How would Wally know where to go? But he'd saved her life before and she was determined not to doubt him now.

Wally lunged forward and Emery held on, trying to follow where he led without weighing him down. The muscular dog guided her around what must be the coffee table, though she could not see it, and past the lumpy sofa.

Wally plowed on, cleaving through the smoke until they reached the front door. She unlocked the bolt and they crawled into the darkness.

The pristine air was delicious, cooling to her overheated face.

Ian, her mind shrilled. She hadn't heard him cry through the whole ordeal. Her stomach clenched into a fist. What if...?

Roman exited right behind her, helped her to her feet and continued urging her forward until they reached his Bronco. Both of them heaved in lungfuls of clean air as he guided her into the passenger seat and handed the baby into her eager arms. She peeled away the blanket, breath held.

Ian blinked at her, his breathing normal and color fine as best she could tell. He whimpered and squirmed and she'd never been so happy to hear him fuss.

"He's okay," she breathed.

Roman's shoulders sagged. "Thank you, God."

She could only nod in silent agreement, cuddling the baby close. She fought tears, pressing kisses to Ian's forehead in spite of his wriggling.

Roman touched her. "And you are too, Ree?"

The press of his fingers made more tears crowd her eyes. She nodded and forced out a breath. "A-okay."

He bent and kissed her forehead, trailing a finger over her tearstained cheek. If he hadn't been there... But it was more than gratitude and relief. For one frightening moment she felt such a flood of affection for him, it was as though her anger and disappointment with him had all but disappeared.

Confused, she could only huddle there, against his chest, and wonder until he pulled away.

He locked her door and closed it. Going around to the driver's side, he started the engine, flipping on the heater. "Do you have a phone with you?"

She shook her head. "It's on the bedside table."

"Take mine. Call emergency and then the ranch. It's programmed in. My sister or Mom will answer. Tell them what happened and if I'm not back in ten minutes, they need to send backup."

"Where are you going?"

He trotted to the porch and grabbed the jacket Gino had left there. "To look for Gino. He might be on the grounds, out for a walk, or in the garage. If there's trouble, if anyone approaches, drive away from here."

Trouble? More trouble than her father's cabin burning down? The grim reality spread through her consciousness. Someone had locked Roman in the basement, her in the bedroom and set the place aflame while she was sleeping, hoping she would die. The baby too?

Before she could ask anything else, Roman closed the door. Through wisps of smoke, she saw him bend down and offer the jacket to Wally for a sniff.

"Find," he said.

Without hesitation, Wally beelined, not for the house but into the night.

Emery's whole body went cold as she soothed the baby.

If Wally hadn't alerted, they all might have died in the fire.

Out in the darkness, would Roman and Wally encounter the person who'd set it?

Clutching the baby, eyes trained into the night, she prayed.

Officer Hagerty arrived on scene and took a report. It became clear that the culprit had entered through the rear of the house after breaking the side window. Roman talked to Hagerty a few feet from the Bronco where Emery sat with the baby. His expression was grim. "Seems someone really wants her dead," he said.

"Someone who knew where to find her, how to get in. Waited until I was in the basement, maybe."

Hagerty was quiet. "Gino?"

"I don't know for sure, but it's odd that we can't find him at the moment. And there's the missing iPad, which he had easy access to."

"Yes," Roman said.

"If this involves the Taylor family…" Hagerty held up a rough palm, "And I'm only saying if… We should look at it through the three big motives…money, power, love."

Roman thought aloud. "Taylors might have money problems—certainly Lincoln created a mess when he betrayed his wife with Diane. Emery said Mason told her Lincoln is a poor businessman."

"And maybe the brothers are in a power squabble over the car collection, but none of those motives indicate why Emery Duncan would be in the crosshairs."

"That's the problem I keep running into also."

Hagerty stuck his pen in his breast pocket. "Enough for now. I gotta talk to the fire chief."

Roman hustled back to the Bronco with Wally. Emery did not argue this time when he drove them back to the ranch. How could she? The fire department had contained the fire but the house was a sooty mess. They would be able to salvage some things, probably, but certainly not until the building was cleared and the smoke had dissipated.

One firefighter had graciously located the bottles of formula in the fridge and delivered those to Emery along with a package of diapers and a handful of tiny clothes he'd been able to save. In her gratitude, she'd almost cried.

"We'll get whatever you need," Roman said as they drove to the ranch.

She turned a stricken face in his direction. "What about Gino? Where could he be? He hasn't answered my phone calls or texts. I'm really worried."

"We'll find him." Roman hoped his words conveyed more optimism than he felt. Gino could not be unaware of what had happened. If he'd been in the vicinity, he'd have heard the cacophony of sirens and responded. Unless he couldn't...or didn't want to.

He set that thought aside and ushered Emery and Ian into the house where Beth waited. "I borrowed a porta crib from the neighbors and Kara helped me set it up."

Kara nodded shyly. "We zipped out to the store and bought more formula and bottles too. Roman told us what kind."

Emery looked on the verge of tears again. Reluctantly he watched her disappear into the bedroom.

Garrett clapped him on the shoulder. "Done all you can for one night. Party starts early tomorrow. Better get some shut-eye."

"I'll sleep on the couch in here, instead of my trailer," he announced.

His brother arched a brow but didn't comment.

Wally slunk to the fireplace and made himself comfortable on the carpet. Not like he would be upset about staying inside instead of in his kennel, and Roman had the overwhelming need for them both to be close to Emery and Ian.

He was glad his brother hadn't asked why.

Because he couldn't have explained it, anyway.

TWELVE

The morning came all too quickly. Roman gathered his family before Emery emerged from the bedroom. "I know it's a lot to ask, but I don't want Emery alone, even for a moment."

"You worried Gino's behind this?" Stephanie said.

He scowled. "I don't know but someone wants her dead and I don't trust the guy."

"Why would Gino want to get rid of Emery when he's been helping her care for the baby all this time?" Kara distributed mugs of coffee.

Garrett, always affectionate, squeezed Kara's arm in gratitude. "He might have motives we know nothing about. Can you look him up, sis? See if anything jumps out at you?"

"Sure." Kara's fingers were already tapping away.

Ian's crying filtered through the door and Garrett lowered his voice. "In the meantime, there are enough of us around. One of us will have eyes on her and the baby."

Reassured, Roman and Stephanie let their dogs out for exploration time in the yard. Garrett helped Kara and his mom set a table outside with the agreed upon coffee, lemonade and cookies for whoever arrived for a tour of the ranch before the main event.

Maybe no one would come, he thought in a panic as the time ticked by. He'd overestimated the appeal of a combined dog and car program. It would be a flop. What had he been thinking? Taking such a risk with their minimal funds? The midmorning sunlight did not warm away the ice in his gut. At the sound of approaching vehicles, Wally glanced up from the hole he was excavating.

Roman plastered on a pleasant smile and let himself out of the gated yard. He watched the first car roll up, the black Mercedes with Mason and Lincoln.

"We ready?" was all Lincoln said.

"Absolutely." *Please, let us be ready.*

Mason snatched two cookies, waving away his brother's objection. "I know, I know. I shouldn't be eating cookies since I'm unable to exercise at the moment, but we can't all be fitness machines and you rushed me out the door." He took a bite and jutted his chin at Roman. "Rumor has it Theo Duncan's place burned last night."

Roman watched the two brothers for any sign that they had inside information but Mason was his usual friendly self and Lincoln was unreadable. "Rumors spread fast."

"Faster than a six-minute mile," Mason agreed. "What's going on? The fire, someone throwing rocks?"

"I don't know."

Lincoln scowled. "You don't know, or you won't say?"

I wouldn't tell you either way. He wasn't sure exactly where his dislike of the Taylors sprang from. Until recently he'd looked at them strictly as business partners. But what if one of them was involved in threatening Emery?

Roman was saved from breaking the awkward silence when Hilary showed up in a large van along with a dozen guests from the inn. Four of the arrivals were women, jauntily outfitted. They chattered cheerfully. The men headed straight for the coffee. Lincoln strolled toward the women.

"There goes Romeo. Doesn't take him long, does it?" Mason sighed and wiped his hands. "I'd better do my part to grease the skids with the men. Happy visitors are more likely to open up their wallets and purchase classic cars aren't they?"

"How many are you looking to sell?"

"Five would break even for what Lincoln spent on the showroom, but that'd be a stretch."

"Overextended?" Why had he said that? Absolutely inappropriate.

Mason stiffened. "Who isn't?" His penetrating look seemed to laser right through Roman. Truth. He'd overextended Security Hounds too, hadn't he?

Mason shrugged and relaxed. "Cars are expensive investments. Even rich people are content with window-shopping, it seems." He beamed at a bewildered-looking man with a leather jacket and boots. "Duty calls."

Officer Hagerty arrived and chatted with Lincoln and Mason before he sought out Roman. "Accelerant, fire department confirms. They're still sifting through the debris." He nodded to Emery who'd come out on the porch, holding Ian.

"This might not be much encouragement, but the department is ready to release your vehicle, Miss Duncan."

Emery's hair was glossy in the sunshine. Her smile was tired, but bright nonetheless. "That's something, anyway. Thank you."

"Got a few folks from the police board and county officials here amongst the visitors," Hagerty said. "You and the dogs gotta shine, Wolfe."

He tried to keep the tension from his voice. "We're ready."

Hagerty gave a mock salute and wandered into the crowd.

"You're going to be great," Emery said. "I promised Wally a pacifier if he tried super hard."

He laughed, ridiculously pleased at her optimistic tease. "That should do it." He bent to tickle Ian's cheek, gratified as the baby gave him a gummy grin. "And you'll be pulling for us, won't you, baby boy?"

"We both are," Emery said quietly.

He embraced her, both of them, heedless of the gathering group. It felt so right. The urge to kiss her rolled over him, but Stephanie had climbed up on the porch and commanded attention. She introduced Chloe and Wally and taught a mini lesson on the attributes of the bloodhound. The guests appeared to be interested, he was thrilled to note, and peppered them with questions.

"And you'll see the dogs in action from the big-screen live feed at the showroom," she said. "Lincoln's enlisted the help of…?" She looked at the crowd.

"Me, Vivian," an attractive blonde said, shooting up her hand. "All for a good cause, right?"

Lincoln grinned at her. Roman noted Hilary's glower. He could see that Emery had noticed too. Romeo, indeed.

"Yes," Mason piped up. "It's for a great cause. Taylor Autos is donating ten percent of all our proceeds this weekend toward funding a local search and rescue team. We appreciate your participation, Vivian."

"Happy to help," the woman said, but her gaze was still on Lincoln.

Stephanie nodded. "Lincoln and Vivian will make their way to the car…"

"The beautiful Bel Air our employee has brought over and hidden, disclosing the location only to me," Mason added in dramatic fashion.

Stephanie smiled. "They'll hike over to the car and hide inside. Our hounds, Chloe and Wally, will track Vivian's scent, using her glove."

Vivian held it aloft for all to see.

"But before that, we'll whisk the rest of you right off to the showroom and you can follow the dog's progress via Chloe's Go Cam," Hilary said. Her tone was cheerful but she stared daggers at Lincoln. "Has everyone finished with their snacks and gotten to meet the dogs?"

Mason provided the location to Lincoln and Vivian who set off immediately.

After a half hour, the visitors loaded up and drove off for the showroom. Roman returned to his dog and massaged Wally's ears. "Ready to rumble, Walls?"

Beth and Officer Hagerty climbed into the ATV.

"Mom…" Roman started.

She held up a "don't even try it" finger. "We're not going to miss this." He was surprised when Emery settled in the tiny rear seat after Kara took Ian from her.

His uber shy sister joggled the baby and began to coo at him. They'd be secure on the property with Garrett who was staying behind in case anything went wrong or they needed another dog. And as far as Emery's safety went, with Hagerty accompanying them, he didn't see how the situation could be much improved. He and Stephanie donned their Security Hounds vests and checked their gear. They gave the dogs a good hydrating drink and a few jerky treats they used only during missions.

A half hour later, Hilary texted that the guests were assembled in the showroom for the live feed. Steph activated Chloe's Go Cam and they attached the long leads to the harnesses.

"Ready or not, here we come," Stephanie said.

The dogs were enthusiastic as Stephanie offered them both a deep whiff of Vivian's glove nestled in a plastic bag. A few moments to soak in the scent, and a loud command to "find" and the dogs were eager to go.

They hustled off, not stopping to reconsider the smells as they did when they were uncertain. Roman's heart raced. Maybe, just maybe, this plan would work. Since he was sprinting to keep up with Wally, he was soon hot and sweating, struggling to keep from tripping on the rocky ground. Trees and thick foliage were not a problem for the bloodhound bulldozers, but Roman was glad he'd worn his heavy-duty pants and boots. Even so, he took a branch to the face that made his eyes water.

The ATV was out of view since it had to keep to the more level trail. Five minutes stretched to ten, then twenty. Excellent. It needed to be a long enough mission to keep the remote viewers interested.

Down a brushy gully they went. They stopped the dogs for a rest period, watered and gave them a treat and reassured them of the scent. Chloe leaped up at the end of the break, but Wally trailed off toward the far end of the gully, which was almost completely swamped in shrubbery, way too small a space to hide a vehicle.

"Wally," he said sternly. "Find."

Wally continued to strain away from the departing Chloe and Steph.

Stephanie turned and tossed him the scent bag. "Try to redirect. I'll keep going."

He nodded, remembering ruefully that all the guests would now have seen footage of his dog going on a walk-

about. On the trail above him, he saw the ATV, the glint
of binoculars. Three more sets of eyes trained on his location. He wished they would keep going, follow Chloe, not
his wandering hound.

It took all his strength to pull the dog to a stop and put
him into a sit. When he opened the scent bag to refocus
him, Wally used the opportunity to take off in an all-out
sprint for the shrubs. Roman barely caught the end of the
lead. Thankfully that hadn't been caught on the Go Cam.

"Wally," Roman shouted. Of all the times for the dog to
go after a squirrel or rat, this had to be the worst. Why had
he thought Wally was ready for a public mission?

He ran in pursuit.

In the far distance he heard Chloe's joyous baying, loud
as a trumpet blast as she neared her target. He hauled on
the leash, but trying to pull Wally to a stop was like trying
to harness a freight train. There was no help for it but to
let the dog follow his trail until he got it out of his system.
At least Chloe had saved their skins.

The dog stopped abruptly. Roman was able to catch up.

He had just started in on his tongue lashing when he
saw what his dog had been after.

The toe of a boot pointed up at the sky.

Heart sinking, he grabbed his phone.

Emery stared through the binoculars as Hagerty dropped
his, leaped from the ATV and disappeared over the rim of
the gully.

What had he seen? What had Roman found?

When she got the lenses into focus, her heart stopped.

She didn't hear what Beth shouted, nor thought out a
plan. She simply tumbled from the ATV and prayed that
she'd been mistaken. Pulse slamming, breath heaving, she

scrambled down the slope, heedless of the dirt infiltrating her shoes and socks.

Roman held up a palm as she approached as if to stop her. Despite him, she collapsed to her knees next to Gino's crumpled form. Blood smeared his forehead and his leg was twisted at an odd angle.

"He's alive." Roman's words finally penetrated.

She took Gino's fingers in hers. Cold, so cold. "Oh, Gino," she whispered. "It's Emery. Can you hear me?"

Hagerty talked quietly on his radio. Roman took a knee next to her, touching Gino's wrist.

Gino's eye cracked open. "You shouldn't be here."

Emery leaned close. "It's all right. You're going to be okay."

He stirred, winced.

"Stay still." She blinked back tears. "Help is coming."

"How'd you'd get here, Mr. Kavanaugh?" Hagerty said.

"Dunno," Gino rasped. "I was at Theo's. Heard a noise and went outside to check. Someone hit me over the head, went through my pockets, my phone. I think they thought I was dead when they dumped me."

Emery stroked his arm. "Don't try to talk. It's okay."

He shook his head, sending the leaves in his hair scattering. "Need to tell you. Should have before."

She was going to stop him again, but Roman caught her eye and she pressed her lips together.

"I've been keeping something from you," Gino said. "Something big." He was talking so low they both knelt to hear. Hagerty edged closer.

"We're listening," Roman said.

He breathed in and out, shallow and pained. "I love Diane...have since the eighth grade. When she blew back into town with a baby... I was stunned. I dove right back into the best friend role. Figured I still had a shot, if things didn't work out with Ian's father." He groaned. "Never should have let her go to the Taylors alone. I thought Lincoln would boot her right out but he let her stay there. I kept telling her something wasn't right. He didn't want the baby, or her, wouldn't even take a paternity test."

And certainly his ex-wife didn't want Diane and Ian around, Emery thought. But what had Gino been keeping from her? And why? And who could have left him for dead?

Roman frowned. "You've been lying to Emery? About what?"

He blinked, wriggled, eyes on Emery. "Your dad asked me to keep you out of it. I promised I would."

"My dad?" Nerves flared up and down her spine. Her father had been keeping secrets with Gino?

Gino blew out a deep breath. "Theo didn't shoot Mason," he croaked. "Diane did, but your father believes it was self-defense. That Lincoln arranged to meet her and murder her by shoving her over the balcony rather than marry her. Her text convinced Theo she'd been threatened somehow. That night... Theo thinks Diane was lured to the house where Lincoln was waiting and she shot the gun to protect herself but got Mason instead before she fell."

She gaped. "Lincoln wasn't even on the property that night according to the police report."

"Your dad sensed there was someone else there in the upstairs hallway. He thinks it was Lincoln but he knew no one would believe it." Gino gulped. "That was Theo's mission. Take the fall for Diane and use his time in prison to prove Lincoln set Diane up to kill her. He couldn't afford a private eye so I was helping."

Hagerty was hanging on every word. Emery hadn't realized Beth had joined them until she squeezed Emery's shoulder. "Ambulance will be here in a few minutes."

Emery's mind was reeling. Her father hadn't shot Mason. Diane had, but it was self-defense? And he was working to prove Lincoln intended to murder Diane?

Roman looked incredulous. "But Theo's fingerprints were on that gun."

Gino took a shuddery breath. "Theo told me he arrived on the property to find the front door open and Diane lying on the bottom floor with the gun still in her hand. He checked her, heard a groan from upstairs, ran to find Mason shot. He realized Diane would be sent to jail so he wiped the gun and left his own prints, fired once more into the floor to be sure he'd test positive for GSR. He had to hurry back to Diane so he couldn't take time to search the property, but he was certain there was someone there. Figured it was Lincoln since Diane said in her text she was all wrong and scared."

Emery realized she was squeezing his wrist so she relaxed her grip.

Hagerty asked permission to record with his cell phone. "So what proof has Theo been pursuing to incriminate Lincoln?"

Gino closed his eyes, breathing hard. "His location that night. If he could catch Lincoln lying about his whereabouts, the police might investigate further."

Emery couldn't follow. "How?"

"The fitness tracker. Lincoln wears one all the time. He's a fanatic, Diane told Theo when she called him the day before the shooting. Always wanted the newest and best model. Even wore it when he was asleep. Your dad asked me to see if I could hack into Lincoln's fitness tracker account."

Emery could only gape in surprise. "A fitness tracker?"

Beth nodded. "I get it. I have one also. It not only monitors your steps but your location too. It's got a GPS in it."

"Which would prove Lincoln was at home when his brother was shot," Emery finished. "That he'd been lying."

Gino shivered and Emery chafed his arm.

"The info only stays for thirty days on the device, but it's stored on the website until it's erased," he said faintly. "Theo figured if I could hack into the account, he'd have enough to at least convince the cops to open an investigation. Maybe serve a warrant and discover threatening messages from Lincoln to Diane."

"Info acquired by hacking isn't going to put Lincoln away," Hagerty said. "And we're not going to get a warrant with hacked information either."

Roman frowned. "Maybe Theo was hoping to put pressure on Lincoln and force him to confess to threatening Diane."

Emery sank back. "All this time, you've been working with my dad while he's been in jail and neither of you ever said a word."

"Yeah." His smile was faint. "Trying to be some kind of Dick Tracy hacker. Lincoln's sign-in was easy but I've not been able to figure out the passcode."

"And to repeat, that's illegal," Hagerty said.

"I know. Emery, I think there's someone in the jail feeding Lincoln info about your dad's calls and visitors. All the danger lately… Lincoln must suspect your dad is onto him, and that he might have shared some of his suspicions with you. He could have been the one spying on us, burgling the mail at your apartment. I think he set the fire too…did this to me to try to get me out of the way. Could be when he knew you were coming to town, he panicked, tried to drown you to prevent you from returning and stirring it all up again. Or to suppress any proof Theo might have passed on to you."

"The iPad?" Roman said.

Gino sighed. "Mine. Snuck into the basement to do some research and accidently left it there when Emery saw it. I was looking at it when I was attacked and now it's gone."

Emery bit back a groan. "There is no proof in the cabin or anywhere. Only speculation. All this is for nothing. Why did Dad tell me to go home, anyway?"

"I wondered that too. I'd told him I thought I was being followed and the mail had been gone through. He must have gotten scared. He'd heard about Security Hounds. Maybe he wanted you to get help from the Wolfes since I couldn't crack the case."

Roman's eyes went wide.

Gino squeezed her hand. "I'm sorry I lied to you. I never should have agreed. Should have stopped you from returning in the first place but I didn't know how without spilling everything."

It made sense now, how he'd tried to talk her out of going, offering to come with her to Whisper Valley. "It's okay," she forced herself to say. "You were trying to help my family. Right now, all that matters is getting you to a hospital."

The rescue crew arrived and Roman assisted them in strapping Gino to a stretcher.

Before he was moved, Hagerty leaned in. "Not approving what you did, Mr. Kavanaugh, but for the sake of Emery and Ian's safety, don't talk to anyone. I'll see what we can do to keep this between us until I've got some evidence to move on. Got me?"

Gino nodded.

Emery could only give him one more squeeze before he was hauled up and out and driven away.

She stood on shaky legs, trying to process. Should she feel hopeful? Angry? Worried? All of the above? If Lincoln was the one who had threatened Diane and left Gino for dead, what would happen once he figured out Gino was alive?

"Will he be safe?" she said to Hagerty.

"I'll see to it. I'll roll with the ambulance to the hospital and make sure."

He climbed out of the ravine.

Wally poked her thigh. She cradled his squishy head. "Wally, you found him." She looked at Roman and Beth. "I know it wasn't what you'd hoped, but Gino might have died without Wally."

Roman's smile was half pleasure, half chagrin. "Typical Wally. He chooses his own mission."

But she knew the dog's deviation might reflect badly on Security Hounds. Everyone was paying the price for what had happened at the Taylor estate on that terrible night.

Roman consulted his phone. "Chloe finished. The guests were impressed."

Beth bent with a twinge of discomfort and patted the dog. "See? All is well. Nothing to worry about."

Her stomach knotted. Nothing to worry about...unless Lincoln had really threatened Diane and escaped looking completely blameless. Was he trying to kill Emery now too because of her father's prying?

Was he the reason her sister was in a coma and her father in jail?

From Roman's distracted demeanor as he collected Wally's leash, she knew he was wondering the same thing.

He took her hand and she clutched his warm fingers.

"You were right about your dad," he said.

"He was right about you too," she said, throat thick.

Tears blurred her vision. She should have been filled with relief.

Instead all she felt was fear.

THIRTEEN

Stephanie and Chloe returned late afternoon, aglow. Roman felt a thrill that part one of their business plan had gone brilliantly, in spite of Wally's detour rescue. Roman eyed his family seated around them. His mom, Kara sitting cross-legged with her iPad in her lap, the twins Stephanie and Garrett. Emery stood by the sliding door, hugging herself. It should have been a celebratory moment. Instead his body hummed with the aftermath of Gino's rescue.

Gino's confession was so farfetched, wildly improbable. Lincoln had been trying to lure Diane to her death? Simply proving Lincoln was on the property that night wouldn't necessarily convince the police to investigate. But what if? What if they were actually partnering with a man who'd planned to murder Diane? Gino? Emery?

He snagged a look at Emery, quiet, troubled.

Theo wasn't what Roman and everyone else thought him to be. Guilt chewed at Roman. What if all this time his mentor had been sacrificing himself for his daughter? That was consistent with the man Roman knew or thought he did. He'd believed Theo to be a man of service, compassion, courage.

And maybe that's exactly what he was. A thought stabbed at him. If Roman had gone to see Theo in jail, showed the slightest sign of support, maybe Theo would have broken his silence and come to Security Hounds for help.

Water under the bridge. Right now, Theo could be depending on them to save his daughter.

He caught Emery's gaze and smiled.

She offered one in return.

Hagerty's arrival interrupted.

"How's Gino?" Emery asked.

Hagerty accepted coffee from Beth. "He's stable, with a broken leg and a concussion. I've asked the hospital to state only that he's under sedation, not to divulge the severity of his injuries. He's got an officer posted at the hospital door."

Stephanie frowned. "Gino's story is so convoluted. If Lincoln is guilty, why would he risk everything to kill Diane just to avoid a paternity test? He doesn't have to marry her, only meet his responsibility to support their child if Ian is his. Murder seems extreme."

"Murder is extreme," Kara said, without looking up from her computer.

Roman resisted the urge to pace. "Okay, let's say hypothetically Lincoln did do it for that reason. And he's lying about being off the property altogether. Did he have help or is he acting alone?"

"Hilary? Mason?" Garrett tapped a pencil on the coffee table. "Those are the two likeliest coconspirators. His ex-wife doesn't have much good to say about Lincoln, so would she aid and abet?"

Stephanie frowned. "She might if Diane planned to force a court paternity test. Revenge might be enough motivation for her to want Diane dead."

Garrett nodded. "Okay. What about Mason?"

"Maybe he's got a motive too," Stephanie said. "Diane

shows up and Lincoln's forced to pay child support. Lincoln's already imperiled the car business with his spending. Maybe Mason sees a way to stop him? Or maybe if Diane marries Lincoln, it affects a will or something and Mason loses out."

Officer Hagerty settled onto the love seat with Wally crammed as close to his side as the dog could manage. The object of Wally's interest was Hagerty's leather belt. Leather was one of Wally's two favorite items. Good thing he didn't carry pacifiers around or Wally would have never let him get up off the furniture.

Hagerty stroked the dog's ear. "You all see how this looks though, right? A man jailed for attempted murder is eager to pin the blame on someone else. An upstanding citizen, I might add, who's bringing business and tourists to the area." He narrowed his eyes at Roman. "As the voice of the law here, I need to remind you all that Theo confessed to shooting Mason Taylor and he hasn't offered one word to the contrary except what we've heard from Gino. Not generally how an innocent man would behave, is it?"

The room fell into an uneasy silence.

Unable to stand still a moment longer, Roman got up and rolled his shoulders. "I agree it's wild that Theo thought he could prove Lincoln's guilt from jail. That he'd allow himself to be arrested rather than reveal his suspicions to the cops."

"It's not." Emery's statement blasted through his thoughts.

He blinked. "But having Gino try to hack into the fitness app? It's ridiculous to think that would work."

"He would do it to protect me and Diane."

He saw the beginning of her tears and realized he'd wounded her. "I didn't mean…"

"It's not ridiculous or farfetched. Don't talk about him like that. Now that I know how he's been trying to find evidence…" Her lips trembled. "He sacrificed for us, gave up everything." One tear slid down her cheek, and before he could say another word, she got up and banged through the porch door.

He looked at his family. "Was what I said that bad?"

Garrett shrugged. "Doesn't matter what you said. Matters how she feels about it."

He closed his mouth and walked outside. She stood near the fence, watching the dogs, arms folded around herself like a bulletproof vest.

"I'm sorry, Ree."

She didn't answer, didn't look at him. "Deep down you don't really believe he's innocent."

"It's not that…"

She turned on him. "Because you don't want to believe it, do you? You still want him to be punished because he disappointed you."

"No."

"Yes." Her eyes flashed. "You want punishment because you want him to hurt like you were hurt."

He had no idea how to reply. "Emery, I loved your dad, but…"

"Loved? Past tense?" Her eyes glittered. "That's at the bottom of it, isn't it? You were hurt, by your birth mom, by what happened with Jax and now my father. You won't forgive them. Maybe deep down you think if you let go of that anger, you'll discover you aren't worth loving? Punishment is better than vulnerability, right?"

Anger stirred in his belly. What did she know about what he'd experienced? The scars it left behind? "Maybe this isn't about me. Maybe it's you that's angry for what your family set in motion. You had to take in your sister's baby after she train-wrecked herself. You said she made messes her whole life that you had to clean up and here you are doing it again. Now you're going to forget all that?"

She smacked the fence post. "I haven't forgotten it. I live with the unfairness of that every single sleepless night, each exhausting day and every moment in between."

"How?" And in that moment it seemed as if he'd never wanted to know an answer so badly in his entire life. How did she live with the circumstances thrust upon her?

She dashed at the tears with her sleeve and let out a breath that sagged her shoulders and seemed to drain away her anger. "God set me on the diving board and said, all right, Ree. I've loved and forgiven you all your life. Now I'm asking if you can do the same by forgiving your sister and loving Ian."

"And you answered yes."

"I'm trying to. Every day." Her words were high and choked. "I wasn't there for my sister because I was angry at her and happy to dump it all on my dad. That's the truth, I'm embarrassed to say. Now I'm trying to show up like I should have done then."

The catch in her voice cut at him and he longed to take her in his arms but he wasn't sure where he stood, where they stood. Instead he simply stared at her, willing his mouth to fashion words around his feelings. Nothing came.

Emery exhaled, her shoulders slumping. Slowly her chin came up. "Roman, I don't know how everything has gotten to this point, but one thing I'm sure of. You have to look in the mirror and decide you're worth loving because God said so and He's the only one that's going to do it perfectly. No man, or woman, can deliver." She turned that blue-green gaze on him and it took his breath away. "I think you're worth loving and so did my father. I'm sure he still does."

She walked slowly away, into the house, leaving him open-mouthed.

He sought the solace of his trailer. Flopping down in the chair, his mind buzzed with uncertainty. Theo, Emery, Eli. Pain from his past rushed through him in an angry tumult. The photos in his bedside drawer called to him and he pulled them out, two of very few photos he possessed.

His sister Stephanie's nickname for him was the Photo Fugitive. True, he had a visceral reaction to having his picture taken, a fact that the women he'd dated in and out of the service had found off-putting.

No fun.

Party pooper.

Wet blanket.

He'd heard all their remarks.

Roman fingered the photos.

Gonna hurt. Why look?

But he did, anyway. In the first he was a gangly teen with spotty skin, grossly overdue for a visit to the barbershop, grinning up at Uncle Jax, similarly unkempt, muscular from his days working on various rigs and pipelines. It was his own expression that got him, the love in it, the trust he'd given so willingly.

It had hurt so profoundly, like a bullet punching through his rib cage, when Uncle Jax introduced him to Melissa and her three kids. One older than him, two younger, a whirlwind of soccer trophies, straight-A report cards, a pending college scholarship. Roman had handled it terribly. Jealous, reactionary, finding fault with the woman who tried to discipline him until Uncle Jax tearfully told him to straighten up or get out.

He'd left.

Over the years Jax had called and he'd ignored the messages, at first out of hurt that Jax had brought in a whole new family, but then out of shame at his own behavior.

He drew the one from underneath.

An older Roman, starting to fill out with muscles, his hair cut military short, though it would be another year before he enlisted. This time he was standing beside Theo Duncan, the man who'd helped him sort out his own anger into manageable portions, set him on the road to honorable military service, screwed his head on straight enough that he could accept love from him and the Wolfes.

Try as he might, he could not see anything but gentleness in Theo's face.

I would still love my father even if he was guilty.

Emery's pronouncement had stunned him.

Love doesn't turn on and off like that. It doesn't with God and it shouldn't with us.

Yet Roman had turned his off tightly, sealing it closed. The images of Jax and Theo showed him flawed men, with a mixture of strengths and weaknesses instead of the caricatures he'd reduced them to.

Uncle Jax the Betrayer.

Theo Duncan the Murderous Hypocrite.

The photos came into clearer focus, two men who had offered love and acceptance to a lonely youngster. Jax and Theo had both loved him generously, offered what they could.

You have to look in the mirror and decide you're worth loving because God said so and He's the only one that's going to do it perfectly. No man, or woman, can deliver, Roman. Only God.

He closed his eyes, sank to the floor, back pressed to the mattress, praying as the tears began to fall.

At sunrise, Emery tapped on Roman's trailer door. Wally stood at her shin, tail swinging, paws muddy.

Roman looked from her to his dog. "Did you dig your way out of the kennel again?"

Wally didn't wait for an answer but pushed in and snuffled around the kitchen in search of crumbs.

She'd had a whole speech planned out, calm and controlled. Instead everything evaporated the moment Roman opened the door. "I'm so sorry. I was horrible to say those things to you." And then the tears started in again, fountaining out of control.

He didn't reply, simply reached out and guided her inside before wrapping her in an embrace. "No apologies," he said over her sniffles. "You were right. I needed to hear it. Probably I've needed to for a long time."

She clung to him, feeling the beat of his heart against her cheek. When she raised her tear-stained face to his, he closed the distance and kissed her. There was a river of sweetness in that kiss that warmed and soothed her, circled around the aching places in her soul like a healing balm. They'd both sustained so many wounds, upheavals, violent u turns, but here they were together and she wondered for a moment if that's what God had intended all along.

But he eased her away and into a chair and her daydream floated away. Friendly understanding, nothing more. She attempted a calm smile, wiping her tears with the tissue he offered. She saw the photos taped to the refrigerator, Roman and a man who had to be his uncle, Roman and her father. He caught her look.

"They're two important men in my life," he said. "No matter how things turned out."

The sun crept through the tiny kitchen window and straight into her heart.

He cleared his throat and shuffled to the kitchen, poured a bowl of water for Wally. "Thought I'd maybe call Uncle Jax later after the event is over." He didn't look directly at her when he said it but she caught the shine in his eyes, anyway.

"I think that's fantastic."

Several silent moments ticked away between them. Roman fiddled with the blinds. "How is Gino?"

Emery wiped her eyes. "He's holding his own. He has to be very still and quiet to give his brain a chance to recover from the concussion. His leg will heal fine, the doctor said."

Wally slurped water, sending it sloshing over the floor, which made her laugh. "Is he going to have a role today?"

"Considering he went rogue yesterday? We'll let Chloe take the lead again, but Wally will be on the premises to answer questions and meet and greet."

She steeled her spine. The moment had arrived. "Roman, I want to come with you today."

He jerked. "Uh, no. I don't think so."

"I have to see it, the place where it all happened. To try to make sense of it in my mind. This is my only opportunity."

"Emery…"

"I'm not being irresponsible. I know someone is determined to kill me and if Dad is right about Lincoln, I'll be walking right into his home, but Hagerty will be there and you and Stephanie and Garrett and all the guests. Very public. Very safe. Kara will stay with Ian again and there will a police officer checking periodically."

Roman heaved out a breath and rested his hands on his

hips. "You've thought this all out. I get the sense whatever I say is going to be a waste of breath."

"That's about the size of it."

He shook his head. "You're as stubborn as Wally."

She laughed and headed for the door, but part of her spirit lagged.

His kiss had made her feel loved, she realized, in a way she'd never experienced before.

But it hadn't meant the same to him, clearly.

"Something else?" he asked.

No, nothing else. "Um, no. I'll see you later."

She kept her smile bright anyway, the rising sun chasing the shadows away as she returned to the ranch house.

FOURTEEN

Emery. Roman simply could not get her out of his mind. The kiss, her tears of remorse, the peace she'd prompted him to accept that felt like putting down an anvil he'd been straining to hold for more than a decade. It left him off balance, confused.

"You're adding to the chaos."

Garrett's voice snapped him out of his reverie, along with the rivulets of water Wally was shaking off from the bath he'd just received. Wally trundled a safe distance away from the hose and shook violently again.

Roman laughed at the dripping dog. "You aren't the best at obedience, but at least you're clean." The dog sent Roman a look of pique.

Chloe received similar treatments before they were loaded up into the special trailer Roman had painstakingly converted for their use with comfortable stalls that opened onto ramps from the outside for ease of loading and unloading. He climbed aboard and followed Stephanie and Emery in one vehicle and Garrett and Beth in the other.

On the porch Kara joggled Ian and waved the tiny baby's hand at them as if he were sending them off. They wouldn't be alone. Hagerty had, indeed, posted a cop at the end of the drive and Roman appreciated the precaution. It didn't quite ease all the tension away. Emery's safety, the event's success, Beth's pain, all weighed heavily as they made the journey to the Taylor estate.

Several pristine classic cars were visible, parked on the grounds to the side of the main house and guests were strolling around them, sipping and snacking. The show-room itself was set back from the fence line, all glass and sleek angles, the doors propped open to encourage visitors inside. They'd agreed on a staging area for the dogs under a cluster of towering pines. Garrett set up an information table with Security Hounds flyers and business cards. It didn't take long for the dogs to attract some people. Chloe basked in the attention. Wally surprised him by hanging back, close to Emery. Roman had made sure she was securely situated near his elbow as he fielded questions and kept an eye on the proceedings. Apparently, Wally had decided she needed canine protection. At least on that priority they agreed.

Good dog, Walls.

Lincoln gathered his flock of visitors with a hearty, "Are we living the life, or what?" There was general laughter and a chorus of approval from the crowd. Vivian, the blonde who had hidden in the car, let loose with an enthusiastic "woo-hoo" that got her a thumbs-up from Lincoln.

Hilary wandered toward them. "We'll get the demo started after Lincoln's done being the rock star."

"Seems like a natural born salesman to me," Garrett said amiably. Roman recognized his brother's technique. People would tell Garrett anything because he was the textbook example of approachability.

"A natural born salesman but not a businessman, or a faithful husband, of course." Hilary's words dripped with bitterness and she cast a hostile glance at Emery.

Emery lifted her chin. "I'm sorry for what my sister and Lincoln did and how it affected your marriage."

"Not affected, ruined."

Emery's face reddened, but she didn't reply.

Hilary's gaze narrowed as she looked away. "Mason is more of a man than Lincoln. The car collection would have been in much better hands with him but their daddy never bothered to update his will after Mason was born. A charming procrastinator, and he passed all those genes down to Lincoln." She shook her head. "Anyway, don't know why I'm dumping all this on you. Let me see if I can rein in Mr. Charming and we'll select another volunteer to hide in one of the cars. Dogs ready?"

"Yes," Stephanie said. "This will be a piece of cake for Chloe."

Hilary left without another word.

They all exchanged looks. So Lincoln had inherited and never arranged to legally share the wealth with Mason? He wondered what Lincoln's financial arrangement with Hilary had been upon their divorce.

Stephanie harnessed Chloe and waited for the scent article.

"So we've got Lothario Lincoln holding the purse strings," Garrett said. "That's interesting."

"And don't forget the scorned wife, and perhaps a resentful younger brother," Beth added.

"An unhappy family for sure." Roman was grateful once more that God had given him a second chance and he intended to do the best he could for his family, and to try to repair what he'd damaged with Uncle Jax. He'd wasted too much time already. He unfolded a card chair. "Sit down, Mom. Please."

She obeyed with a pat to his hand. "All right. I'll hold down the fort."

He looked over at Emery. "I know you want to see inside the main house."

She flushed. "I was thinking it's a good time for me to visit the powder room."

"Wally and I will walk you over."

"I was hoping you'd say that." She smiled, which added that little dimple to one side of her mouth. He remembered the kiss in his trailer, soft and tender. A fond gesture only, wasn't it? Purely his instinct to comfort? He was still mulling it over, inert with the confusion of it when she squared her shoulders and headed toward the main house. He decided to let his instincts take over for a while and managed to snag her hand, holding Wally's leash in the other.

"I can imagine this is going to be difficult for you, seeing the place where it all happened."

Her mouth was tight as she nodded. "I need to do it for both of them."

He squeezed her fingers, awed at her courage. He'd dismissed his uncle and all the past mess because it hurt too much to face, and here she was, walking right to the place where her family had been demolished. Amazing, that's what she was.

They entered the foyer, which featured a massive spiral staircase in black-and-white marble leading to the upper floor. The lower-level featured a round table housing a flower arrangement and in the corner a bay window flanked by a massive potted tree. Paned windows flooded the room with light.

"Best behavior, Walls," he whispered. The last thing he needed was Wally running rampant. Emery still held his hand, but her skin had grown cold.

"Living the life for sure, aren't they?" His half-hearted attempt to lighten the mood.

She didn't appear to hear, her gaze riveted on the upper-story railing. "They must have replaced it after she…"

After Diane fell.

When he heard her breath catch, he moved to her side, letting the leash out so Wally could explore within limits. He beelined to the indoor tree. "No peeing," he cautioned.

Emery was still staring. Her words came out singsong, as if she were telling herself a story. "Diane was scared of someone so she took her gun to the Taylors' house. She encountered Mason upstairs. It was dark. She fired. Mason was struck and she fell. My dad arrived and found Diane downstairs. He ran to the top floor and discovered Mason bleeding, heard someone else on the premises. He returned to Diane, wiped her prints off the gun and added his own."

"And then he confessed." Roman rewound the tape in his mind. "But your father's theory that Lincoln scared Diane, lured her over there somehow, it's all just conjecture."

Emery sighed. "Lincoln probably discarded the tracker already and deleted the account."

"Possible."

"Then we have nothing." She sagged. "My dad might not survive, nor my sister. Even if I did figure out the website password and the account is still active, the evidence wouldn't be admissible. I don't know why I thought coming here would make any difference."

Her defeat felt like a physical blow. Security Hounds hadn't been able to help, nor had he. Wally pawed at the heavy terra-cotta pot. Through an interior doorway, a woman entered in a housekeeping uniform. She headed straight for them.

"I'm sorry, sir. You can't have a dog in here."

"He's a working dog. We're here for the demo." Wally didn't help Roman's case by trailing a ribbon of saliva down the side of the pot and whining.

"I'm sorry, sir," she said firmly. "No dogs."

"It's okay," Emery said. "I'll visit the powder room and come right out."

"We'll wait for you on the porch," Roman said. "Use the front door only, right?"

She nodded. "No wandering, no exiting through a rear door. I know."

He lugged Wally to the shaded front steps. In the distance he could hear a sudden ripple of excitement from the showroom. Chloe must be doing her thing. The murmur rose to a cheer and he silently added his own. "You'll get there someday too, Walls." The dog was far too annoyed at being pulled from his potted plant to listen.

His phone buzzed, a group text to all of them from Garrett.

Guess what? With the police department's blessing, a county administrator has officially offered Security Hounds a trial search and rescue contract.

Roman pumped a fist in the air. He realized the only person he was burning to tell was Emery.

Emery emerged from the restroom to find the housekeeper gone. She gazed around the pristine flower-scented space. Living the life. Would her family ever be able to do that? Whatever secrets this room contained, they would remain there forever. She started for the front door, distracted by the dark patch of Wally's drool on the terra-cotta pot. Why had the dog been so interested?

She gazed up at the balcony one more time, imagining it giving way, the failure sending debris raining down from the upper floor. A strange thought occurred to her. What if…?

She hurried to the plant and looked all around its mossy base. Nothing there. Of course not. What had she expected? Still, the urge for further examination needled her. After making sure the housekeeper hadn't returned, she knelt next to the pot and shoved her arm into the dark space. Her fingertips met only slick tile. Hunkered down, she stretched a few inches farther and touched a pliable rubber object. Quickly she snatched it out of its cubbyhole.

Unable to believe it, she stared down at the exercise tracker with the half-detached wristband. It had to be Lincoln's. Nerves zinging, she quickly wrapped it in a clean tissue from her pocket, praying she hadn't ruined any evidence. "Roman," she called as she got to her feet.

A hand clamped over her nose and mouth, an arm cinching around her neck. She tried to struggle, scream but the grip was fierce. Sparks danced before her eyes.

Roman…

Her shoes skidded uselessly on the slippery tile.

The pressure on her windpipe increased.

She couldn't make a sound as she was dragged away.

Too long. Now that the euphoria of Garrett's text was fading, Roman became more aware of the time.

The visitors were spilling out of the showroom and Emery still hadn't exited the house. He shoved open the door. There was no one in the foyer. Heedless of annoying the housekeeper, he and Wally burst inside and raced down the hallway that led to the powder room. No sign of Emery.

He was about to shout for her when Wally nosed hard at

something and barked. It was one of their flyers, crumpled. Emery had dropped it. He knew it in his bones. He knelt next to the dog and offered him a proper sniff.

"Find," he said. *Please, Wally.*

The dog launched down the hallway. They raced past rooms, which Wally ignored completely, until they burst into an enormous kitchen. A caterer arrived one moment after them, holding an empty tray, startled. "Can I help you?"

"Did you see someone come through here? A dark-haired woman?"

"No, I was out with the guests."

Roman plowed through the exit door, which funneled him into a well-tended backyard. He clutched his phone as Wally dragged him across the grass toward a cement sidewalk.

"Garrett, Emery's gone. Lincoln must have snatched her from the main house."

"Not Lincoln," Garrett snapped.

"What?"

"I'm looking right at Lincoln and Hilary. Not them."

He gaped. "Can you see Mason?"

"Negative."

His blood ran cold. "He's our guy. I'm heading west with Wally tracking. Get Hagerty."

"Copy that."

Garrett would locate the cop, but by the time he caught up, it would be too late for Emery. He didn't know why Mason would have snatched her. Something to do with his inheritance or protecting his brother? Either way, if he was desperate enough to try an abduction in a public place, he wouldn't let her live. Wally galloped along the cement sidewalk. Roman rushed as fast as he could to keep up.

Unless he overtook Mason, there would be no last-minute rescues this time.

* * *

Emery swam to consciousness, her thoughts jumbled, her throat raw where he'd choked her. Her senses cleared and she realized she was in the rear of a car; she'd been dumped into the back seat. Her ankles were bound with duct tape. Not again. She managed to wriggle to a half-sitting position but her hands had been taped with messy loops to the passenger headrest and tugging only compacted the strips into wiry ropes that cut into her skin. How much time had passed? Would Roman have noticed?

"Lincoln, please," she called into the front seat. "I won't tell if you let me go."

"About the exercise tracker you found behind the plant?"

Wrong voice. It hit her like a brick. It wasn't Lincoln who'd abducted her.

"I simply could not figure out where it had gotten to," Mason said. "Even without it, your dad was getting close. I have a friend who works in the jail who told me Theo was poking around, asking someone he called to contact companies that sell fitness trackers. I figured he was talking to you." His tone was chatty, friendly. "When he had the heart attack, he mumbled something about proof. I assumed it was something he'd mailed you or spoken to you about. I would have liked to kill him then but it's hard to get to someone in a prison hospital, so I decided to get rid of you and the potential proof. I stole your mail once but whatever he sent is bound to arrive sometime and I can't stake out your mailbox forever."

Her father was truly innocent. All this time she'd known it and now it was confirmed. "He didn't tell me or send me anything."

Mason shrugged. "Too late now, isn't it? No one would believe him if he does happen to recover, but they might believe you. So…" He grinned at her in the rearview mirror. "When the drowning failed, I decided I could get you at the inn. That was a bust."

"So you tried to burn down my dad's cabin? Attacked Gino?"

He shook his head. "I didn't know that Gino clod was working with your dad until I heard him on the phone outside your cabin. He was chatting with a fitness-tracker company, trying to convince them he needed to recover a lost password, so I took action. He was supposed to die in that ravine. I never planned on any of this. It snowballed. I had to act before it was all gone."

"What?"

He lifted a shoulder. "Everything. The cars, house, showroom. Dad left all the assets in Lincoln's name and never revised his will when I was born. Oh, sure, my brother was going to get around to making things equitable like Dad intended. Every year he'd mention it, and did he ever follow through? Of course not. There are too many slackers in this world."

She slowly put the pieces together. "Lincoln cut you out of the assets."

"Not purposefully. He's a procrastinator like my dad but he also doesn't know how to run a business, or a marriage for that matter. Between alimony and dithering around with the cars, I'll be fortunate to have anything left when he does sign half over to me, which he's been promising to do for the last thirty years."

She could hardly make herself believe it. Mason was the exact opposite of the friendly community-minded local he'd pretended to be. "I won't tell anyone anything. I'll leave with Ian. I promise." She hoped her voice didn't quiver.

Mason didn't appear to hear. "Theo's false confession was too easy. I knew he had something planned, that weasel."

The right crime, the wrong man. Mason, not Lincoln, all this time. "You're wrong, Mason. My dad thought Lincoln lured Diane to the house to kill her."

He didn't answer for a moment. "If only I'd known that. I was the one who got her to come that night."

"Why?"

"To kill her, of course."

Emery shivered. "I don't understand why you'd risk committing murder."

"Lincoln decided to take that paternity test. He was going to find out Ian was his and marry Diane. He always felt bad that his infidelity ended things with Hilary. That's why he paid for her inn to be remodeled. He said he was going to get it right the next time he married, be the better man. What do you think would have happened to the remainder of the collection if he married a second time? You think I'd ever get my share? Not until after he sold it all off to pay for a wife and kid."

"You figured you'd kill Diane, make it look like a fall?" She continued to flex her hands, stretching the tape a little more. A hot trail of blood oozed down her arms.

"The afternoon it all went down, I followed Diane to her favorite coffee shop. She called your dad, I heard her blabbering about her plans to get together with Lincoln, that he was coming to love Ian, et cetera, et cetera. He was softening on the paternity test idea."

She caught a glimpse of his sly smile in the rearview mirror. "So what exactly did you do, Mason?"

"What I had to."

And now he thought he had to kill her.

Each minute brought them farther out of town, deeper into the wilderness that had almost been her grave before.

Desperately she yanked on the tape.

He wasn't going to get another chance.

She had to find a way to save herself or her father's sacrifice would have been for nothing.

FIFTEEN

Roman was covered in sweat when they emerged at the outbuilding at the end of the walkway.

Wally pawed at the door of the neatly tended garage. It was placed well away from the house, probably designated for employee cars and utility vehicles.

His phone rang.

"Wait until I get there," Hagerty puffed. "Got units responding."

Not waiting. He pocketed the phone. The panel on the roll-up door was a numbered keypad. Kara could undoubtedly crack the code since she loved number puzzles more than breathing but there wasn't time for that either.

Instead, he hustled to the side window, concealed by a curtain. Finding it locked, he put Wally into a sit, picked up a rock from the ground and bashed it through the glass. The hole enabled him to reach in and force the window and drop down inside. He saw immediately where the car had been parked. Slamming the garage opener from the inside, he raced out and texted the group.

He's got her in a vehicle.

Steph's reply popped up immediately. Direction?

"Wait one second." He dropped next to Wally and reminded him of the scent. "This is it, boy. No squirrel chasing or stubbornness. I need you to help us find her. I'm counting on you." Wally's nostrils quivered as he smelled the crumpled flier again. "Find," Roman said.

If they failed...

He shook the thought away. After what seemed like an eternity, Wally decided on a direction, nose glued to the ground. He circled, looped twice and stopped after only a couple of yards. Logical. He'd lost the scent at that point. Even bloodhounds could not track subjects in speeding cars. But it was enough. Had to be.

Northbound, along the frontage road, he texted.

No response dots immediately popped up, and he knew what they were thinking. Was Wally accurate? Should they bank all their resources on it?

He tried to clear his mind. Garrett, head south, in case we're wrong.

Got a unit at the junction, Hagerty texted. He won't get to the freeway.

What was between here and the junction? His heart fell.

The lake. Would he take her there again? Finish what he'd attempted?

His legs felt like rubber. Borrowing a vehicle. Heading north toward the lake with Wally, he messaged.

He felt the thrill of fear in his mother's reply.

Stay safe. He's desperate.

Desperate. Well, so was Roman.

Desperate to capture Mason, make him pay for what he'd done.

Desperate to capture the most radiant light in his world.

Desperate to save her.

He grabbed a nearby motorcycle by the handles and rolled it out of the garage. The keys were in the ignition.

Wally barked and jumped. Roman grabbed a rope and climbed on the seat. The dog's wrinkled face broadcast his fear that he would be left behind.

Not leaving you, Walls. Roman scooted back and patted the space in front of him.

Wally sailed into the spot and Roman awkwardly tethered his companion to him, like a mother carrying her baby. It was ungainly, but it would provide enough protection that Wally wouldn't fall. "I got you, Wally."

He gunned the engine. The dog howled. In a frenzy of noise, they jetted away.

Emery's arms ached from tugging at the tape. She'd almost succeeded in freeing one of her wrists but the car was now bumping and jostling, indicating Mason had driven off the main road. She needed to cover the sound of her yanking.

"Why were you wearing Lincoln's exercise band that night?"

"I took it when he was in the shower before he went out. I used it to send Diane a text, pretending to be Lincoln. Did you know you could message with those things? It said he'd decided to take the paternity test and sue for full custody and he'd win because of her seedy past, that he'd pay people off if necessary to prove she was an unfit mom."

Full custody? How that must have terrified Diane. Ian was the best thing in her life. "My sister thought Lincoln was out to get her but it was you all the time. And everyone thinks you're such a nice guy."

He sighed. "Good plan though. That part worked, she came charging up the stairs. I was going to give her a shove and be done with it. That old railing was weak. No one would know it wasn't an accident. If she didn't die, I could help her along before calling the cops. Never would have guessed that she carried a gun. I took a step toward her and she shot me as I shoved her over. I bled like crazy, but I saw her phone near me. I deleted my text from both the fitness tracker and her cell. No trail back to me. I was in the process of wiping my prints off the exercise band when I got lightheaded and collapsed. Dropped the silly thing."

Emery felt like screaming. It had been Mason all along.

"Your father barreled in but I pretended to be unconscious. His confession to protect Diane worked in my favor. Cops didn't delve too deeply into the details."

They wouldn't. Mason appeared to be the victim and they had a confession.

Her thoughts spun faster and faster. The app could put a person at the scene of the shooting, but it couldn't identify who was actually wearing the exercise band, not without fingerprints. The wristlet she'd found was the smoking gun. It was gone from her pocket, of course. He'd taken it when he'd choked her at the mansion. She held back a groan.

Mason seemed to read her mind. "I didn't think there was any way I could be implicated. That's when it dawned on me that the lost exercise band would have my prints. I couldn't delete the app either because it's in my brother's name and I don't know the password. The only loose end."

His tone was hard; she could barely believe it was the Mason she'd known. A terrible thought dawned in her mind. "Wait a minute. That's your plan B, isn't it? If Dad's sleuthing made the cops reopen the case, or you couldn't get rid of me and whatever proof you thought I might have, you were going to let Lincoln take the fall."

"My first choice was to keep us both out of jail, but..."

He shrugged. "The app was in his name, like I said. It was on the property the night of the shooting. He had a strong motive to want her gone. If he continued to refuse me my fair share of the inheritance, that little tracker would be my insurance policy, providing I could find it. If I did, I'd wipe my prints to clear myself and if necessary, arrange for it to be found by someone else. I'd suddenly remember seeing my brother threatening Diane. The cops would get a warrant and retrieve that deleted text that looked like it came from him. I've been waiting on Lincoln to take care of me for decades and he's ready to jump in with both feet for a woman who isn't even his blood? How much can a man take?"

"You'd sell out your own brother."

"He sold me out first." The car jerked to a stop. Frantically she hauled on the duct tape but she was out of time. He yanked open the door, cut the loops around her wrists and dragged her out by her taped feet. She fell onto the muddy ground, terror ribboning through her.

The lake.

He'd brought her back to drown her.

And this time he wouldn't botch the job.

"They'll know it was you," she panted, getting to her feet.

"I don't think so. I'll cut off the tape after you're dead so it looks like you jumped in yourself, return the car, change clothes and sneak back to the showroom before anyone's the wiser. I'll be just as shocked as everyone else when your body is found. They won't pin it on me."

He held up the wristlet. "But thanks for finding this. Never would have thought it could have landed behind that potted tree." Before his smile had time to dim, she shoved him as hard as she could. He cried out, doubling over, the wristlet flying from his fingers. She grabbed it and hopped frantically away. Hide. She had to hide or maybe outpace him if she could.

"Stop," he shouted.

She was at the edge of the trees, hopping, leaping, throwing herself into the covering foliage. Slithering as deep as she could into the branches, she searched for a sharp rock. Thorns and branches tore at her, but she located a stone with a jagged edge. Immediately she sawed it against the ankle tape. It began to give way, but Mason was staggering toward the bushes now, muttering. She saw glimpses of his genteel face, twisted in hatred, his neatly cut hair mussed along with his clothes.

Hurry.

One more inch of tape to go. She sawed for all she was worth until it came loose. Then she was up and running, slapping at the branches that barred her way. If it meant surviving, she could run like this forever and Mason was recovering from a gunshot wound. She'd make it. She'd…

And then a shot whistled by her cheek. She turned, stopped dead at the sight of the gun in his hand.

He smiled. "Diane was smart to carry a weapon. Took a page from her book, so to speak."

A sob escaped her and Mason offered a sad smile.

"I'm sorry it had to work out this way."

She pressed her lips together. She wasn't going to beg. Ever.

As she closed her eyes, the roar of an engine swept over her. Roman appeared on a motorcycle with Wally tucked against his stomach, heading straight for Mason.

Mason held up the gun to fire. Emery hurled the rock she still clutched. It deflected off Mason's temple and he fell.

When he rolled over to get the gun, Roman slid the bike

to a stop, freed Wally and leaped off, diving onto Mason. It was a short battle, punctuated by Wally's ear-splitting bays and howls as he darted around the men.

Finally Roman turned Mason over onto his stomach and knelt on his lower back.

Wally trotted over to Emery and slobbered all over her with his massive tongue.

Roman's frantic gaze found her, sirens wailing in the distance. "Emery…"

She struggled to breathe. "I'm okay. You did it. You two tracked me."

He smiled and nodded. "Piece of cake," he panted.

Wally howled.

She felt like sobbing, but instead she laughed.

Roman sat in the waiting area of the county hospital while Emery visited her father. Theo's prognosis was guarded but improving. There were subtle indications her sister might be showing signs of recovery as well. Lots of prayer and a long road ahead for both of them, he thought.

His fingers still tingled from the last text he'd sent.

Uncle Jax, been doing a lot of thinking. Can I talk to you sometime?

The reply popped up within sixty seconds.

Absolutely. So glad to hear from you, Baby Boy. You name the place and time.

He smiled at the tiny screen.

Gino had insisted on watching the baby while they visited the hospital, hobbling around with Kara's help, his foot encased in a cast.

Emery came out and he held her, let her wipe her eyes before he guided her into the Bronco. They drove to a peaceful spot, a grassy meadow fringed by trees, far away from the lake. He'd brought a picnic for them, a bowl of treats for Wally.

They sat on the blanket and chatted, eating their sandwiches while Wally meandered around, reveling in the scents.

"This is the perfect way to spend an afternoon," she said. "After everything that's happened."

"I still can't believe Mason was behind it all."

She shivered and he snuggled her closer. "And the horrible thing is, my father didn't have any proof and hadn't sent me anything or even told me his suspicions. Gino couldn't hack into Lincoln's account. Mason might have gotten away with everything if he hadn't decided to go after me."

Roman exhaled. "I don't want to think about Mason right now."

"Me neither."

But he knew it would take a long time to get past what had happened, for him, but mostly for her. They focused on the picnic, enjoying the breeze that whispered across the grass. She enjoyed his offering, humble peanut butter and jelly though it was. When they were done, he ceremoniously presented her with an empty ice-cream cone and pulled a scooper from his jacket pocket. "I am finally keeping my promise."

She chuckled, the light in her face igniting joy in his heart.

"Ice cream?" she said. "I knew you were good for it."

He opened the cooler with a flourish. In shock, he did

a double take. "Wait. What?" He spun around. Across the meadow, Wally sat with his purloined strawberry ice cream, slurping from the container he'd torn in half for better access.

"Wally," he shouted. "This is abominable. You are grounded for the next year of your life. Do you hear me, dog?"

He turned back to find Emery laughing so hard she was unable to speak. In a matter of moments he was breathless with laughter too. They guffawed until the tears ran free and they were both out of breath. "Aww man. I'm real sorry about the ice cream."

Her cheeks were rosy. "Honestly, I think there is nothing better in this world than a bloodhound."

"Almost nothing."

She looked a question at him.

"I mean this." He gestured to the landscape. Words bubbled out, in fits and spurts. "All this beauty, being able to live here, with a family." He tried to calm himself. "And having you in my life again, and the things you've taught me."

She quirked a brow. "Me?"

His stomach tightened. "Uh-huh."

"But I haven't taught you anything."

"Yes, you have." He took her hand. "How to hold a baby, the power of a pacifier…"

She giggled. "That's nothing."

He swallowed a lump in his throat. "You taught me that God loves me no matter how I blunder, just like you love your father."

Her eyes went wide.

He pressed on. "You said you'd love him guilty or not. Reminded me that's the way love is supposed to be, not conditional, not something that ends when someone disappoints you." His throat felt tight again. "I texted Uncle Jax. I'm sure he'll let me know it's taken me a dog's age to realize what I should have known all along."

She grinned, a brilliant smile, and reached to put her palms on his cheeks. "I'm absolutely thrilled that you're talking to Jax."

He pressed her hands in his and drew them to his lips for a kiss. "Me too. We're going to meet soon."

"That's fantastic, Roman. Really wonderful."

He paused, touching his cheek to her fingers, not daring to look her in the eye. "Want to come?"

She hesitated, confused. "Of course, if you want me to, but isn't that a family moment?"

"Yes, it is." He looked at her and inhaled until his ribs creaked. "And I want you to be my family."

Her mouth opened. "Your...family?"

"Yes, ma'am. I love you." He gripped her hand. "I love you, Emery. I don't ever want to lose you again."

Tears glistened under her lashes and she stared at their joined fingers. And then he heard it, the smallest of whispers that shouted louder than a blast of thunder. "I love you too, Roman."

For a moment he couldn't move at the sheer joy that was so overwhelming it bordered on pain. "I'm sorry I wasn't there for you earlier. When I think of how..."

She squeezed until he stopped talking. "Let's go forward, not backward. We've learned and moved and grown. Tomorrow's more important than yesterday, right?"

"Right."

"Forward," he said. "As long as I get to spend my tomorrows with you."

She bit her lip and eased from his grip. "But it's not the right time."

His spirit plummeted. "What do you mean?"

She hung her head and her voice dropped to a whisper. "My life is a mess. The police will have to unravel all the threats before Dad is exonerated. His cabin needs to be dealt with, and my sister's care is ongoing. And Ian... He needs so much. It wasn't what I chose, but he has to be my first priority now."

His spirit filled with pride at her commitment, her love for others.

"I'm in."

"You're in? For all that? The mess and the baby and—"

He kissed her until she stopped talking. "I'll try to be the best uncle I can to Ian, like Uncle Jax tried with me."

Her expression was still somber, but wondrous too. "I know you will, but..."

"And when your sister is better..."

"That's just it. She might never be," Emery said in a strangled voice. "If she can't take care of Ian, then I will be his mom and whoever marries me..."

"Will be a stepdad."

"Yes." She looked at him half-fearfully.

Last he'd heard, the distraught Lincoln had professed some sort of interest in staying connected with his son. That wasn't enough, not nearly. The boy didn't need a connection; he needed a "boots on the ground" dad. "Like I said, I'm in."

Now the corner of her mouth lifted a tiny bit. "Are you sure?"

He stroked her cheek with a finger. "If that's how it works out, I'll be the best father I can be to him. I don't know a ton about parenting, but Uncle Jax can advise and

Beth is the epitome of an amazing parent. They'll help me learn and so will you. Whatever it takes. I don't know how, exactly, but I'll make sure Ian always knows he's loved by me, and by God." He swallowed a swell of emotion. "Period."

He leaned in and kissed her and the sensation of unbridled joy consumed him again. Her response told him she believed him. She would belong to him and he to her and through their mistakes, blunders, missteps, they'd hold on to that bond that God had given them and try to instill it in Ian.

Tears splashed down her cheeks and she flung her arms around his neck and kissed him. "Roman, I can't imagine my life without you."

"Me neither," he said with a cocky smile. "In every photo I'm gonna be right there with you and Ian too." He kissed her again.

Wally finished licking the ice-cream container and yowled.

Emery produced something from her pocket, which set Wally's tail wagging.

"May I?" she said to Roman.

Roman laughed. "He doesn't deserve it. He's just consumed an entire pint of stolen ice cream."

"A treat, for all he's done for me."

"Wally come over here, you disobedient bloodhound," Roman said. The dog cast aside the empty container and sauntered over without a trace of guilt.

"Sit," Emery told him.

He did.

She held out the shiny red pacifier.

Wally almost knocked himself over in his eagerness to accept it. He licked and sniffed and snuggled it between his two massive front paws until they were both breathless from laughing.

Emery took a selfie of the three of them together. He found he didn't mind at all having his picture taken this time. He pressed her cheek with a kiss in the next one.

Wally whined in happiness.

"It wouldn't be a family picture without Wally," she said.

Roman chuckled. "I suppose he'll worm his way into every photo now."

As if he realized he was being talked about, Wally woofed.

"But no more pacifiers, Walls," he said sternly.

"At least not when anyone's looking." Emery smiled slyly as she slid another one from her pocket. Wally perked up as if he'd heard the dinner bell ringing. "This one's blue. Totally different flavor. No harm in a little spoiling is there, Mr. Wolfe?"

He laughed loud and long before he swept her into another embrace.

"No harm at all."

* * * * *

*If you enjoyed this first book in Dana Mentink's
new Security Hounds miniseries,
look for more books in this series
coming soon!*

And be sure to pick up
Trapped in Yosemite,
*a full-length romantic suspense novel
by Dana Mentink, available now
from Love Inspired Trade!*

Dear Reader,

Bloodhounds! The more I learn about them, the more amazed I become. Did you know that bloodhounds have the best scent receptors of any dog breed? They can out sniff even the beagle and the basset hound. Bloodhounds have been known to stick to a trail for more than 130 miles. Incredible, right? So it's exciting to be kicking off a series about a private detective agency that relies on bloodhounds to help solve their cases.

Of course, bloodhounds can occasionally lean to the naughty side. Case in point is Wally, who loves his pacifiers and sometimes snatches a meal without being invited. I hope you enjoyed meeting Wally. In the course of the series, you'll also get to know Chloe, Tank and Pinkerton and their human companions, the Wolfe family.

Thanks for coming along on the journey! If you'd like to connect further, you can reach out and contact me via my website at danamentink.com.

God bless,
Dana Mentink